Diane Bvholt
125
Por

327

MW01463432

HELLBENT KID

HELLBENT KID

Gordon R. McLean

CREATION HOUSE
CAROL STREAM, ILLINOIS

© 1973 by Creation House. All rights reserved. Printed in the United States of America. Published by Creation House, 499 Gundersen Drive, Carol Stream, Illinois 60187.

Library of Congress Catalog Card Number: 73-86950

International Standard Book Number: 0-88419-065-X

To
Frank Ubhaus, Ben Escobar, Jr., Dan Poley

Three friends who gave so much to help a young man find the Way.

Foreword

On the road, the Minnesota Twins and many other ball clubs arrange weekly chapel programs wherever we happen to be around the country. At one of those programs our guest was a young man you will get to know well as you read these pages, Art DePeralta. Art shared very simply and honestly the problems he had encountered in life and how he also had come to realize that pleasures could not give him the answer to life for which he was searching.

Several of our fellows mentioned the courage he had to stand up and bare his soul to us. We have all committed wrongs that do not make the front pages of newspapers, but in God's eyes are still sins against Him. I could relate to Art's story even though I have never experienced the same trouble with the law as he did. You do not have to rob a bank or peddle dope to be guilty in God's sight.

There was little similarity between the lifestyle of the young man speaking and this ballplayer listening to him. And yet, in his own way, each of us has needs which only God can meet. We also share the sense of forgiveness, inner peace, security and satisfaction that come from a life centered in Christ.

And that is what this book is all about—a new life through the Lord. I'm thankful for it in my own life. I'm glad Art is getting started in it, too.

Jim Kaat

Preface

When I read in the papers the tragic story of how two young men terrorized a crowded bank, then led thirty police cars on a dangerous chase, I was as shocked and angry as the next guy. I didn't know in a few days I would meet one of them, become his friend, and that the court would ask me to assume daily responsibility for his supervision while he was returned to the community for nearly six months, awaiting court actions.

During that time, I got to know Art, his family, and his friends well. And I watched a young man struggle with his own sense of shame, his desire to do better, the changes in his thinking, the happy moments and the deep depressions. I saw the faith at work in his life that turned it around. I watched him get so discouraged he was ready to forget the progress he had made, go out and get in trouble, or simply ask to be locked up again. But no matter how tough things got—or how miserable—he never quit. One step at a time, he learned to walk in a new life. By the time he came to court for sentencing he was not the same young man who had made headlines six months earlier.

You'll meet Art on these pages. Yet it was never his intention or mine to write a book about him. But so many things kept happening that seemed worth sharing, and most people who met him asked questions that almost demanded this form of answer. This book would never have been possible without some generous assistance from the federal and county probation departments, the Federal Bureau of Investigation, the public defender's office, Wells Fargo Bank, and the many individuals mentioned on these pages.

My special thanks go to Jim Kaat, now of the Chicago White Sox, for his kind introduction to this book and his friendship to Art during tense days; to Dr. Gordon S. Jaeck, social scientist; to Drs. Larry Turpen and Jerry Dickson; and to Irv Brendlinger, Oklahoma City youth minister, who gave valuable counsel and assistance; to Grace Francone, who typed the manuscript; to Clyde Vandeburg of Vandeburg-Linkletter Associates in Hollywood who arranged for publication; to *Campus Life* and *Christian Life* magazines for use of my material they originally published; and to the *San Jose Mercury-News* for their photographs.

All Scripture quotations on these pages are from *The Way*, an illustrated edition of *The Living Bible*, as developed by the editors of *Campus Life* magazine.

Finally, the hero of this book is *not* a young man who went out and got into serious trouble, but rather the One who made a difference in that young man's life. I commend Him to you.

Gordon R. McLean
1190 Lincoln Ave.
San Jose, Calif. 95125

November 30

The bullet ripped into the floor with a crack that instantly got the attention of startled tellers and customers.

They turned to face two young men, masked, wearing surgical gloves. The shot had come from the younger man's .357 single action Magnum revolver as the pair came through the front door of Wells Fargo Bank on Alum Rock Avenue.

The other man, a 9mm automatic in his hand and another gun in his hip pocket, yelled for everybody to get up and away from their desks. His accomplice headed for the assistant manager while ordering everyone else down on hands and knees. One employee got the front of her dress ripped when she didn't move fast enough; a loan officer was kicked. The older robber began to fill pillow cases with stacks of money, more than two hundred thirty thousand dollars in all. (One bag was dropped on the way out, however, so the final take was just over one hundred nineteen thousand. It was the largest robbery in the history of San Jose, California.)

Meanwhile, a bank officer upstairs in the coffee room heard the commotion. He walked over to the landing, peeked downstairs and saw what was happening. He activated an alarm, then slipped down a fire escape and went two doors to a delicatessen where he phoned police.

The frustrated robbers were getting more angry and profane by the second. Their getaway driver was supposed to have pulled up to the back entrance of the bank and come in to help them get the money. He was nowhere in sight.

"Dammit, where's Butch?" Jesse, the older robber, said to Art.

"How the hell would I know? He's supposed to be in here by now."

Jesse went back to check the vault again. Art followed him, looking out a window as he walked. "Jesse, there's cops out there!" Jesse rushed to the front door and yelled out, telling the police to split, otherwise somebody was going to get killed. He fired a couple of shots. Then he told Art to get a hostage. Art grabbed a young teller. "How are we going to get away if there's no car?" Art yelled. There was no answer.

He looked around and spotted a green Chevy parked in the back. "Who owns this car back here?" he demanded. A man stood up and said, "I do."

"Get out there and start it and hurry up," Art ordered.

Turning to the crowd of people in the back by the vault, Jesse called, "One of you girls come over here." He pointed out one lady; she came over. Together the robbers made their way to the car, using the terrified young women as shields.

Outside, a police officer advanced on the bank with a shotgun until someone shouted, "Get back! Get back!" and fired at him. The officer retreated as the men and hostages piled into the car they had commandeered.

"There was no way to get a clear shot at them without endangering the girls," the officer said later.

With the young teller driving, the muzzle of Art's revolver leveled at her head, the wild chase began to crisscross the south end of the city.

The bandits learned quickly they had more problems than the thirty highway patrol, sheriff and police cars plus a helicopter who were tailing them. The gas gauge read empty. (It was broken, but they had no way of knowing.) They began frenzied dashes in and out of gas stations. Attendants scattered wildly each time as the Chevy roared in, followed closely by a pack of police vehicles with sirens screaming.

No attendant, no matter how eager for business, was about to wait on that car! Art even waved a hundred-dollar bill in one station. He still got no service. One officer said the suspects let fly a few bullets in at least two of the stations but no one was injured.

Inside the car, Art asked Jesse where they should be going. The only answer: "Anywhere."

The hostages were terrified. Art was not happy either. The job had not gone right. The girl at the wheel kept screaming that they were going to kill her. He turned to Jesse and said, "Let's surrender, man, we're caught now."

The response was a flat no. Jesse got the lady in back to calm down, and the two actually talked amiably for much of the wild ride.

Art had no intention of hurting the young woman in front, and said so, but of course there was no way she would believe that. Flashing through his mind were thoughts about his mother, and his girlfriend. It was then that he realized he was in a position to take someone's life who had done him no harm. He felt miserable. But there was no backing down. The chase continued.

The police cars lost their quarry for a short time because of some fast turns made at Art's direction. But the helicopter soon spotted them again. After forty miles of chasing, the car finally became stuck while attempting a high-speed U-turn on a highway south of the city.

Dozens of officers converged on the vehicle, guns drawn.

Jesse started screaming that he wanted another car. "Are you going to go for broke with me?" he challenged Art. Art didn't reply.

"Jesse wanted to kill us and shoot it out with the cops," one of the women later told police.

Art didn't want to die, but that was his only

choice other than to surrender. He asked Jesse again to give up. Jesse refused. Art had had enough. He told the woman in the front seat to roll down the window and tell them he was coming out. He threw out his gun, pushed the hostage out, then emerged himself, hands raised. Jesse was yelling, cursing him. Officers swarmed over him.

Jesse then held his hostage in the back seat, her body partly covering his, and put his 9mm automatic to her head. A police marksman crept up from behind. The officer raised his pistol to the right rear window and fired. Jesse slumped over, hit in the forehead.

Before police could frisk him, ambulance attendants pulled him out of the car and headed for the hospital, with a detective riding in the ambulance.

In the emergency room, Jesse tried to reach for the revolver in his hip pocket, but the detective knocked his hand away and took the gun.

Meanwhile Art, who undoubtedly saved everyone's life by surrendering, was taken to police headquarters. Arthur John DePeralta was booked on seven federal charges, including bank robbery and kidnaping, and then state charges. He was seventeen years old.

December 2

Federal authorities announced the arrest of Butch, the getaway driver who failed to show up. He was found in a cabin near Sacramento.

December 3

I was walking down the corridor of Juvenile Hall towards the chaplain's office, which I often use for counseling. Several officers happened to be escorting a young man toward me. Suddenly he spoke.

"You're Gordon McLean, aren't you?"

"Yes," I replied, looking up at the dark-haired, brown-skinned young man before me. I didn't recognize him. "Who are you?"

"I'm Art DePeralta. You don't know me, but you're a friend of my cousin Les."

"Yes, I know Les very well. We've been friends for about four years. And you're his cousin. Where are you going now?"

"The marshals are taking me to a court hearing," he explained, "but it won't take long. Could we talk when I get back?"

"I'll check it out, but I don't see why not. I'll leave word for the marshals to bring you to the chaplain's office."

A short time later there was a knock on the office door. A marshal ushered Art in and left the two of us alone.

We talked some about our mutual friend, his cousin. Then I said, "Art, the officials who talk to you here always begin by telling you of your right to remain silent, to have an attorney present, and that statements you make can be used against you in a court of law. I didn't give you those warnings because here in the chaplain's office it's different. If you choose to talk with me in my capacity as a minister of the Gospel about what you may have done, then our conversation can and will remain confidential. You need to know that."

"I understand very well what you're saying but it isn't necessary," Art responded. "I have nothing to hide. I've told my attorney and the FBI the truth, so there is nothing confidential about it. Frankly I am glad to talk to someone who isn't taking down a statement or something. They're all I've seen in the last few days except for my mother."

I naturally asked him what had happened the day of the robbery. His answers were consistent with the press and television reports. But I was more interested in him as a person than in what he'd done. Of all the kids in serious trouble I've met in more than twenty years of Youth for Christ/Campus Life ministry, I've never met a teenager with the brazen nerve to hold up a bank, kidnap a teller and lead police on a wild chase through city streets.

I had plenty of questions. Why had he decided to rob a bank? Why had the crime been so violent? Where had he learned his cold style? Where had he learned how to handle a gun? What kind of family did he come from? What about his intelligence and interest in school? How did he see himself? What of his future?

I got some answers, but there was no point in rushing. Let him take his time, unwind. Then perhaps the answers will come. And in going slowly I might see a way to minister to him.

I did tell him about my work with YFC's Campus Life high-school clubs, youth guidance counseling with the chaplain at the hall, school programs, my radio phone-in talk show for students and other means of sharing the Good News. Art was interested; he had friends who were in the clubs.

Many of the young people I've met involved in serious trouble with the law have been open and appreciative of any friendship shown them. Finding Art responsive and pleasant was not a surprise, but the extent of his warmth and friendliness was. The reports of the crime had pictured him as a sneering, insolent, even violent person. The young man I met was almost pathetically eager to be pleasant and appreciative of our visit. Granted, that could merely be the front of a youth in serious trouble grasping for any source of help, but I really doubt it. Here is a youth caught up in a serious tragedy far bigger than anything he imagined, and now, in the midst of the crisis, he's at a real turning point. If I'm right, then we're off to a good start that could eventually lead to his whole life turning around. I'll have to see.

Later tonight, Dan Poley, one of the young men on our Youth for Christ staff who's done considerable counseling at Juvenile Hall and the county juvenile ranch, returned with me to meet Art. The two hit it off well. Dan left Art a copy of *The Way*, the Living Bible for students. Art said he would read it.

December 4

Art was in a tense, trying period. "I've got a problem, man," he said. "They keep me isolated in a receiving room. They let me read and take me out for a shower, but that's about all. It's really bugging me."

I knew why Art was in close confinement. Upon admission he had been depressed and had talked of killing himself. Now his mother's visits had lifted his spirits, and self-destruction no longer seemed a threat. But there was no way to predict what he might do in a unit with other young people who might have read about the crime and would badger him with questions.

Then there was the matter of security. When a kid is being held under one hundred thousand dollars bail, his keepers don't take chances.

I explained this to Art. He understood, but then said, "See if I can get into a unit at least part-time. I'm not going anywhere, and this room is driving me nuts." I told him I'd check out the situation again.

Had he read any of *The Way* yet? Yes he had, and he had two books to show Dan and me that he also had been reading: *The Cross and the Switchblade*, by David Wilkerson, and *Run, Baby, Run*, by Nicky Cruz. Both tell the exciting, true story of Wilkerson's work among some of New York's toughest gangs, and how he was able to reach a tough, young street leader whose whole life was turned around when he met the Lord.

The books obviously held Art's attention. They started him thinking new thoughts about God and his own life. He was fascinated when I told him

I knew both Wilkerson and Cruz, and could vouch for the truth of the change in Nicky's life.

"There just might be some hope for me after all," Art said.

December 5

Art's mother had been to see him again. It was obvious, as he told me about it, that he has deep feelings for her. When she first saw him after his arrest, she had assured him of her love in spite of what he had done. She will stand by her son and help him in any way possible. Her support will be strategic if there is to be any redirection in Art's life.

She had brought him some interesting news. Billy Graham had been in the area, read press reports of the bank robbery, and told television newsmen he was praying for all of those involved in the sad event. Art was impressed.

During the day I met Art's attorney, Frank Ubhaus, the assistant federal public defender assigned to the case. Many public defenders are eager, young attorneys looking for courtroom experience and quick advancement into more lucrative private practice. Others are genuinely dedicated to their clients, but are too short-staffed and overloaded with cases to do much for any one of them.

Ubhaus, however, being a federal lawyer rather than a state one, seems to have both the time and resources to give Art his best. He impressed me as being warm, pleasant and capable. He is also confident—which helps when you have to stand in court against the full power of federal investigating agencies and the U.S. attorney's office.

Aside from his duty, Mr. Ubhaus likes Art. So do I.

Dan and I then visited Art's family. His mother, stepfather, four younger brothers and a younger sister all greeted us warmly. They live in a modest home near a large shopping center. Both parents work.

Art's mother summarized the family feeling: "We love Art very much and were all stunned when we learned he had robbed a bank. The comments from kids at school have been hard on his brothers and sister. They didn't want to go to school for a couple of days after. The kids like Art even though he's been away from home a lot, out on his own, with an older group of friends. He never really felt comfortable here at home, and I was concerned about his hours and his associations. But I never dreamed it would come to this. . . ." She just shook her head slowly and did not finish the sentence. She had tried to instill Christian values in her children and seemed to have been fairly successful with all except Art.

"I guess we never got across to him how we felt, or maybe he just couldn't respond. Maybe he felt he was too old, or too independent, or something. He was never rebellious around the house. He just wasn't here very much. I can see some mistakes we've made as well as the ones he's made. Maybe we can solve these problems yet."

December 6

This was the second all-important date in Art's life, even more critical than November 30. Ray Ramsey, who leads the Campus Life club at Art's high school, joined me for the visit today.

Art came to the chaplain's office with some intense feelings and questions. He felt better now that he was spending some time in a unit with other guys. He was getting a little more freedom now since the detention staff trusted him more.

He couldn't get over the change in Nicky Cruz's life as told in the books. The obvious question, which he quickly asked, was, "Would this same thing work for me?"

With Art there were no intellectual games to be played over the authority of the Bible or whether Jesus Christ was God's Son. Nor was he interested in explaining away the deep sense of guilt and shame he felt. Obviously his problem was more than guilt feelings; he had genuine guilt. In fact, he was probably harder on himself than most judges would be.

In addition to forgiveness, Art sought a real change in the direction of his life.

Time flew by, but we hardly seemed to notice. Finally came a decisive question from Art. "Could God *really* forgive me for all the bad things I've done? And remember, you know only a small part of what those things are."

"God already knows, Art. He's known all along," I replied. We found a verse in the Bible: "Those who come to me I will never, never cast out" (John 6:37). "That meant Nicky Cruz, and it means Arthur John DePeralta."

"But how can it happen?"

"Let's get the Lord's Word on that: 'Look! I have been standing at the door and I am constantly knocking. If anyone hears me calling him and opens the door, I will come in . . .'" (Revelation 3:20).

Christ responds to an open door.

I have never understood the divine chemistry that allows a guilty man to humbly invite Christ into his life—and come out of that simple prayer started on a brand-new road. But I know it happens. Today it happened to Art DePeralta, when he prayed a simple prayer asking for the Lord's forgiveness and a fresh start.

Art has still done wrong; he is still locked up facing court and men's judgment. But inside him is a different story! Paul described it nearly twenty centuries ago: "When someone becomes a Christian he becomes a brand new person inside. He is not the same anymore. A new life has begun!" (2 Corinthians 5:17).

A lot has happened to one teenager in a week.

December 7

Today I met Rick—and he is the exact opposite of his brother Art! He's almost unbelievably quiet; he makes honor grades. I doubt he's ever been in trouble in his life. Unlike Art, he has stayed close to the family. The only similarity between the two is a love for sports: Rick in football and Art in wrestling.

As we talked over dinner, I noticed the President's Physical Fitness Award on his jacket. He told me of the work he'd done to earn it. Then we talked about sports and school. Finally the conversation turned to his family and Art. Rick weighed his words carefully, trying not to reflect negatively on Art and yet express his bewilderment.

"Art and I are real close," he said. "He might be gone a lot, but I usually knew where I could get ahold of him. If I had a problem, I would send him word and he'd come around to talk things over with me. He always gave me good advice, even when he wasn't doing so hot himself.

"Art's got a good head. He stays in good shape most of the time. If we'd play around he'd always get me down but he'd never hurt me. He never wanted me or the other kids doing anything wrong. I've never got in trouble but I believe if I ever did I'd have it far worse from Art than with my folks."

And what about the bank robbery?

"I came home from school that day and was lying down when one of my friends from school called and asked if I'd heard about my brother on the news. She said something about a bank robbery and chase. I slammed the phone down and ran out of the house heading for the store down at the corner. When I got there I saw all the headlines and pictures across the front page of the *News* and it was terrible.

"Some kid came up, saw me, laughed, and said, 'Hey, man, that's your brother, isn't it?' I hit him, grabbed my paper and ran home in a daze. I didn't know whether to cry, scream or what—it was horrible. As the other kids came home, I showed it to them. Later my parents came home. They already knew. There wasn't much to say. We were all stunned. We didn't eat much."

I interrupted. "Rick, I know you're close to Art. But there are some big differences between you guys. What about those?"

"I've been closer to the family and I like school better." Rick explained. "There's something else. Two years ago over at our church we had some special youth programs where we talked about accepting the Lord into your life. I did that and now I'm kind of active in church, the sports teams, youth group and teen choir.

"Art never went for that kind of thing and there wasn't much chance for me to get it across to him. He was the big brother and all that. But I have been praying for him that he would find God."

I couldn't help smiling. "Rick, I brought you here to tell you some important news. Your prayers may have just been answered."

"What do you mean?" Rick asked.

"I'll let him tell you. You're going to see him, and soon."

December 8

Dan Poley and I spent some time with Art today going over some portions of *The Way* he had been reading and suggesting ways to grow and mature in the Christian life.

I'm learning that Art doesn't hide his feelings very well. It was obvious today that something was really bothering him. At first he didn't want to talk about it.

"Gordy, there's something bugging me," he said finally.

"What is it?" I didn't know what to expect.

"I've given the FBI a statement about what happened . . . and I told the truth, but I didn't tell all the truth. I left out something very important."

"Do you want to tell me about it?"

"Yes, I think so." I waited. He paused for a minute, bit on his fingernail, looked down at the floor and spoke softly.

"You know about the other two guys. Well, there's a fourth guy they don't know about yet."

"You're kidding. There's somebody else involved here and the FBI doesn't even know about him yet?"

Art looked up and seemed to gain assurance. "There's another man who planned the whole job, got us the weapons and showed us what to do."

"Where was he when the robbery went on?"

"He was supposed to be parked a short distance away with a rifle ready to block any cops coming up on the scene and give us a chance to get away."

"He didn't do that job too well. Why didn't he come in the bank?"

"He couldn't. He's in a wheelchair. He's crippled from a bullet wound."

"Who is he?"

"We call him Big Ben or the Godfather. He was once married to my mother's sister a long time ago. He's been in and out of prison a few times. He taught Jesse, Butch, and me what we know about robbing big places and he set this up."

Dan and I sat quietly as Art struggled with what to do with the information. There was no point in preaching at him just now. He knew the code of the underworld against "ratting"—and he also knew what *The Way* had been telling his conscience.

"Big Ben always said we were a family together. You know, all for one, one for all," Art reasoned.

"Then where was he when you were cornered in the bank?" I asked.

There was no reply as Art fought his inward battle. The surface question was whether he would talk. The real issue was much deeper and Art knew it: Which side was he on? Had he *really* changed? Was he going to do what was right, even if it hurt?

If he talked, his motives would be questioned—by the old crowd, in court, and by the public at large.

"Art, this may sound corny," Dan said, "but what do you think God wants you to do, or even expects you to do, if you're on His team now?"

"I know," Art replied. There was a long pause as Art thought through the implications. "Call my attorney and tell him I want to talk to him."

December 10

Impatient is a mild word to describe Rick while waiting to see his brother today. Both boys—Art in the security section at Juvenile Hall and Rick facing the taunts and questions at school—have been through much in the last ten days.

"My mother told me Art had been really depressed for awhile, but then had come out of it, started getting his head together, and had accepted the Lord. That's hard to believe, Gordie," Rick said when I met him in the lobby of Juvenile Hall. "I'm bewildered. I don't know what to expect."

We went through the security area by the courtroom, buzzed an electrically opened door and were admitted to the receiving area. Then we went to the chaplain's office where Art was waiting. The two guys greeted each other warmly.

"I'm glad to see you, man," Art said. "Sit down and tell me how things are at home." Rick, usually quiet, came quite alive with enthusiasm and shared the interesting bits of family news. Then they talked about what was happening with Art, what he did in the hall, the food, the activities.

Then Art said, "Rick, you and I are really together now. I mean, I did what you did back at the church when you became a Christian. I guess I'm awfully stubborn but I had to get in a real mess before I was willing to ask God to change my life. But I've started on that road now and I see why you're all for it."

Later when it was time to leave, I suggested we pray together. The two brothers shook hands and the three of us thanked God for working His will, even in the midst of tragedy.

"I didn't know a guy could change so much in a few days," Rick said as we left the hall. "He seems happier than I've ever seen him. I *never* thought we'd ever pray together, and the last place I'd think it would happen would be Juvenile Hall.

"Up until now I just thought how bad it was Art got in trouble. Now I can see something good may come out of it, I mean as far as Art changing. It's hard to believe it's all happening."

There were tears in Rick's eyes as he spoke.

December 11

Art enjoyed spending some time down in the unit with other fellows his own age today. He played some ball, watched television, ate with the group, and generally socialized.

But he had one problem.

"Most of the guys know what I'm in for and they came around wanting to talk about the big heist, what was it like, was I scared, didn't I feel like a big man, you know? They want to know if I think I'm all big and bad.

"I can handle myself, but I don't think I'm all big and bad. Sure, it was a big job, but if I'm so blamed smart like they think, how come I'm in here?"

Art repeated what he'd told one guy: "Don't make a hero out of a bank robber; that's just plain stupid."

December 12

A police officer and an FBI agent interviewed Art today. Their investigation had led them to the same conclusion Art had shared with me several days earlier; namely, there were more people involved and more planning to the bank robbery than appeared at first.

Not only did they believe there had been a fourth man involved, but they had learned from other sources who he was and what his role had been. Big Ben was the man they had in mind as instigator of the robbery. Art confirmed that for them. In so doing, he crossed a big hurdle in his personal progress.

He told the truth.

December 13

Art showed me two letters before he mailed them.

The first was to Billy Graham:

When you were in the Bay Area recently on TV news you mentioned a bank robbery in San Jose and said you would pray for the people involved. I am one of those people involved. I was one of those guys who robbed the bank. I was captured after a police chase and shoot-out. One of my accomplices was shot but neither of our two hostages or I were hurt, for which I was thankful.

I am awaiting trial in federal court and may have to spend time in prison, probably a long time in prison. I dread the thought of doing time but I am willing to pay for my mistakes.

I am seventeen and now am in Juvenile Hall. I am really ashamed of hurting the people in the bank and my family by what I have done. While I was here in the hall I met Gordon McLean of Campus Life and he gave me a copy of THE WAY. I have asked the Lord to forgive me and to come into my heart and give me the strength to make the right decisions in the future.

I would like to thank you for your prayers and for thinking of me.

Sincerely yours,

Arthur John DePeralta.

The other letter was addressed to the young bank teller he had taken hostage and held at gunpoint during the chase. He wasn't sure she would get the letter, read it, or even be willing to believe he meant what he said, but he wrote:

What I have to say may not mean much to you, but I want you to know from deep in my heart that

I am really sorry for what I put you through. I am really thankful no harm came to you and we all got out alive.

I have nobody to blame but myself for what I did. I was wrong and I'm going to have to pay for it.

Please tell (the other hostage) that I am sorry for what happened to her as well.

I will be thankful if one of these days the both of you could find a place in your hearts to forgive me.

I have asked the Lord to forgive me and accepted Him into my heart. The best way I can show Him, you and my family I really mean this will be to live a different life in the future. With God's help I am going to do that.

I have been praying for both of you every day and I hope the memory of a terrible experience will not harm your lives in the future.

Sincerely yours,

Arthur J. DePeralta.

I asked him to let me make copies of both letters. He was reluctant, because he considered them very personal. But he finally agreed. Some people would say the letters were glib, the expected penitence of a guy who got caught. In this case, however, I knew that they were both deep and genuine.

December 18

Art went before the U.S. magistrate for a hearing on his bail. Shortly after his arrest, bail had been set at one hundred thousand dollars, an impossible figure for his family to raise. Bail is based on the seriousness of the offense and the possible penalties, which might cause a defendant to flee. Armed bank robbery carries a twenty-five-year maximum sentence plus a ten-thousand-dollar fine, and the kidnaping charges each carry a maximum of ten years to life imprisonment.

A motion had been made to lower the bail. Art was confident it would be granted. After all, things had been going rather well for him.

He was wrong. The motion was denied. Art, dejected, was returned to lockup.

Alone again in his cell, he sat there stunned. He was angry at himself, the magistrate, and the whole situation he had gotten himself into.

But as he thought things through for a while, his attitude changed. He sat on his bunk and talked the situation over with the Lord. "God, You know I wanted out of here and I was pretty mad when I didn't make it. I'm sure not saying I deserve to be out. And I guess You still want me in here to teach me some things and show me that You're in charge. I don't like it, but I'll accept it and make the best of it. You call the plays."

December 19

I returned from a speaking engagement in Chicago and learned of the court action detaining Art. Dan and I talked it over and decided to ask the magistrate if he would reconsider.

We received a courteous hearing. He was relatively young, and listened carefully to what we said. "Do you think Art should be released just so he can be home with his family for Christmas?" he asked me.

"No, I don't. There are many young people who have done much less than he who will be locked up over the holiday. Our reason for urging his release is that he faces a long period of confinement. As it stands now, he will look back only on a career in crime and then being locked up. That can leave plenty of doubt in his mind about the future. But if he has a period of time in the community when he is doing right and living a good life, then maybe he will remember that when he is in prison and realize he can build on a good foundation."

The magistrate listened carefully. "There are strong feelings in the community against releasing Art. I'll make you no promises, but I will hear the matter again tomorrow morning in a rehearing."

If the magistrate had been impressed with my arguments, Dan wasn't. He had gone sound asleep on a chair in the waiting room as the magistrate and I talked!

December 20

At the second bail hearing, Art's mother, the attorney, and an FBI agent were on hand. The marshals brought Art in.

Did the FBI consider Art either a risk to the community in committing more crimes or in fleeing from the area?

No.

Could his parents, who both work, supply proper supervision?

That would be a problem, so we offered to assist both in supervision and in getting him daily to and from school.

"What bond do you want set, and can you provide it even if I do lower the amount?" The magistrate asked.

"Art's parents are willing to post their house as a security that he will make all his court appearances as ordered," Mr. Ubhaus answered, and suggested a figure of twenty-five thousand dollars. Art's mother assured the court that she and her husband had talked it over thoroughly and were willing to back their son.

"Do you realize," said the magistrate, "what your parents are doing for you? They are putting their life savings in the form of their home on the line for you. If you let them down, everything they've worked and saved for could be gone."

"Yes, sir, I do understand," Art responded.

"Then I will grant the request for the bail to be lowered. There will be some conditions. You will be in school every day, unless you are at court or sick. You will be under the supervision of your parents or the Campus Life staff twenty-four hours a day. You will report any threats against you promptly to a federal probation officer, and you will see that officer once a week."

The magistrate may not be too popular with the community and the media for doing that, but it seems fair. After all, the point of bail is not to keep a guy in jail as a form of pre-trial punishment; it is only to guarantee that he shows up in court when he's supposed to. None of the investigators in Art's case doubt that he'll come to court.

It will take a couple of days for the necessary papers to be signed, but Art is going home.

December 22

Today Art, Mr. Ubhaus and FBI special agent Joe Chiaramonte went to the U.S. attorney's office where Art gave a sworn statement that was taken down by a court reporter. Then, with all the questions answered and the papers finally signed, Art was ready for release. Mr. Chiaramonte drove him to his aunt's home where his whole family soon assembled for a happy reunion.

Art called to let me know he was home. "This is the greatest Christmas present I could ever ask for. I never knew just seeing my family again could be so wonderful."

Late in the day, the FBI announced the arrest of Big Ben. His bail was set at $250,000. Bail for Jesse was $200,000, and for Butch $100,000. All four face bank robbery charges: Jesse and Art have additional charges of kidnaping. Trial will come in U.S. Federal Court. Other federal and state charges probably will be dropped.

December 27

Art must return to high school next week. Today I met with a top official of Art's school district to discuss the matter.

Art could not return to their schools, he said. The case had attracted too much notoriety and there might be a strong reaction in the community to his return. Parents have something to say about their son or daughter attending class with a vicious bank robber.

But wasn't Art enrolled in high school?

"Well, not exactly," the official replied, a little embarrassed. "After his arrest we withdrew him. We didn't really expect to see him back."

They would agree, though, to try to get Art in at another high school in a different section of the city. Among educators, this arrangement is informally called "lend-louse"—you take one of our bad guys and we'll take one of yours when needed.

The contact was made and I met with the principal chosen for the dubious pleasure of accepting Art. Not only was Art infamous, but his grades and credits were almost nonexistent. It also appeared from his attendance record he wasn't aware school ran five days a week!

This principal, however, was surprisingly agreeable. "I'll check with my superiors but I believe we can work it out. If he wants to go to school, comes regularly and does his work, he will be welcome here."

There was one interesting provision attached: "We don't want any publicity over the fact he's attending our school. If he's in some meetings or anywhere else in public we'd rather he didn't mention what school he attends. And if you decide to write a book about the case, you can leave it out there, too!"

December 28

There was an unfamiliar, old blue Cadillac parked near Art's home today with two men sitting in it apparently keeping an eye on the place. Later they followed Art when he went out for a drive, but eventually dropped off. He told me about the incident, and neither of us knew what to make of it.

This evening some of Art's old buddies invited him and his girlfriend out for a good time together . . . to renew old acquaintances, or at least that's what they said. Some of the kids were loaded and wanted to get Art either high or drunk. They also wanted to pump him for information about the robbery. As the evening wore on, what had been a tragedy to Art became quite hilarious in the eyes of the group. Art was disgusted and went home early.

January 1

For the last three days Art and two of his brothers were at our Campus Life "Living End" program in the Santa Cruz Mountains. It's quite an event. Seven hundred fifty high-school students with plenty of games, fun, food, and activities to keep them all busy and happy. This year the kids were divided into teams and each was instructed to prepare a short movie script. Then they were given a camera with film and the humorous results were shown in the evening program.

The music of a group called *Gabriel* was both contemporary and alive, but very much geared to communicating. Bob Kraning often followed them with simple, straightforward talks, devoid of religious jargon, telling how a new year can be the beginning of a new life because of the investment God made in sending His Son into the world.

Bob was everywhere on the grounds with the kids. He wound up eating with Art one noon. The story of the robbery came out.

"Did you *really* do that, Art?" Bob asked.

Art was not smiling. "Yes, I did," he replied quietly. "But I know what you've talked about in these meetings because on December 6 I invited the Lord into my life. Without that, I don't think I'd make it at all."

"Would you be willing to share your experience with the group here?" Bob asked. "I think it would be a tremendous encouragement to many of the kids to hear how the Lord changed the life of one young guy. It might help many of them to make the right decision."

Art didn't know about doing that. Public speaking wasn't exactly his line. But if it would help, and if Bob would interview him, well, he would be willing to try it.

That's how it happened that night that a hushed audience listened as one of their own told about a crime they'd all read about in the headlines. But it was more than a crime story come to life. It was an earnest young man seeking not to tell them how bad he had been, but how wonderful was the Lord he had met.

After the meeting, Art and I talked about the experience. "I was nervous up there but I hope it did some good." Then he paused for a moment. "You know I can't remember a New Year's when I wasn't out getting drunk or loaded. This was sure different. And it's the best New Year's I've ever had!"

There were several other young men at the conference who had been in serious trouble. In fact, they had come to the conference from a rehabilitation center and would go back to that facility for a short time before their release. Both fellows had come to know the Lord while in custody, met Art at the conference, shared their experiences with him, and generally were a great encouragement to Art in getting started in a new life style.

John Hafner is a personable, keen fellow who can readily identify with some of the hassles Art faces as a young Christian who still has serious court actions ahead. He told Art the Lord would never get him out of his problems, but would be with him no matter how rough the situation got.

Andy Freedman is an enthusiastic fellow whose sense of humor can pull anybody out of the doldrums, including Art. As a Jewish student who had been heavily into drugs before he met the Lord, Andy is still seeking answers to many questions about his new faith. Art found it very helpful and easy to talk with another fellow who is new at this Christian life and having many of the same growing pains Art himself faces.

January 4

Newspaper men don't often get to interview major criminals. The courts usually don't give them the chance.

Thus when the *San Jose Mercury-News* had opportunity to interview Art, the editors were surprised. It seemed strange that attorney Ubhaus had no objection to an interview. In fact, he had told Art to say whatever he wished about his part in the crime, and that he wouldn't even be present. There was also no court-ordered gag rule.

Art and I went to the newspaper's editorial conference room. The welcome was friendly, but the questions were right to the point.

Question: You are out on bail while the other suspects in this case are still confined and will be until trial. Do you feel you should have such favored treatment?

Art: After my bail was set my attorney made application to have it lowered and that was eventually done. My parents posted the bond and I was released. The other men can make the same requests of the court. I participated fully in what happened and will answer in court as they will. The outcome will be in the hands of a judge and jury.

Question: But do you think you should get easier treatment because you are out, going to school, helping in a Christian youth program, talking in meetings and working on a radio program?

Art: No. Those are things I am doing to help straighten out the mess I've made of my life and to hopefully plan for a better future. They do not change what I have done in the eyes of the law.

Question: You are the youngest person of the

four charged. Will you plead in court that you were led into doing the robbery by the others and you are less responsible for what took place?

Art: No. Others suggested the idea originally and planned it, but I knew exactly what was going on. The choice was mine and mine alone as to whether I would rob the bank. No one forced me. I went in because I wanted my share of what I thought would be a lot of money. I am responsible for what I did.

Question: Do you plan to plead guilty to the charges against you?

Art: I haven't entered a plea yet, but a little later I will and it will be guilty.

Question: You are quite firm in your Christian commitment. Do you see this as grounds for leniency from a judge who may sentence you?

Art: Of course not. Nowhere in the Bible does it say the Lord will get you out of your problems, and I haven't asked Him for that. I have asked Him for the strength to face whatever may be ahead, take whatever punishment may be given, and come out of it a better man, able to make the right choices instead of the wrong ones in the future. I thoroughly expect to go to prison; I deserve it, and I haven't asked God to keep me from it. Paul in the Bible was a lot better Christian than I am, and the Lord certainly didn't keep him out of jail. Why should I expect Him to do more for me?

Question: You were in some trouble and before the Juvenile Court before this case came up. Is there anything they could have done to have prevented this?

Art: Yes. The people at Juvenile Hall are my

friends now; I've been back to see them several times since I got out because I like the counselors. But as far as I am concerned they make a big mistake down there. They keep giving a kid more chances instead of really doing something when he's going downhill. I can see giving a kid a break the first time if the trouble is not too serious, but if he comes back they should see that something needs to be done.

They were thinking of sending me to the county juvenile boys' ranch the last time, but I talked them out of it saying I'd learned my lesson. They sent me home again. They should have known better. Twenty days after being let out for another chance, I robbed the bank. I really think the ranch would have helped me. Of course I didn't want to go there, but it still should have happened.

Question: You didn't do well in school. Why?

Art: School was boring to me. My tenth-grade year was the best because I was wrestling varsity and had some interest. But the classroom routine was a drag. Too many teachers just putting in time giving boring lectures on material I have no interest in, more thought about grades than how much is learned, more concerned about keeping everything calm and easy than getting students enthused about learning. I'm going to switch over to college next month and that ought to be better. I'll have the pressure of the court actions to deal with and I haven't learned to work and study very well, but perhaps I can cut it better than in high school.

January 5

The newspaper has its story, but perhaps not exactly what the editors expected. Far from portraying a rough, young hood, here is material showing a youth frankly admitting his wrong, blaming nobody else, and talking in positive terms about facing what is ahead, then making something good in his future. It's not exactly what the readers expect in a story on a bank robber-kidnaper. And the lawyers for the paper are still afraid advance publicity might prejudice the trial.

The story did not run.

Now that Art is free on bail, it's important whom he spends his time with. He's friendly with some of us in Campus Life, Dan and I are certainly his buddies, but we can't and shouldn't cut him off from all of his old friends, especially those who might be pretty good people.

Art has such a friend. He's Ben Escobar, Jr., the son of Big Ben. Ben, Jr. has not lived with his father since the family split up when he was a small child. Young Ben lived with his mother, went through school, later served a successful tour in the Army, and now is living on his own and holding down a steady job. He and Art are inseparable buddies; in fact, they consider themselves brothers, although Ben, Jr. carefully avoided the worst of what Art got himself into.

January 7

One of Art's responsibilities has been to help produce my Sunday night radio talk show for students on KLIV, a local Top Forty station. He works with my guests as well as talks with the callers before they come on the air to be sure they know the topic and have a clear line. At the end of the program we give our Campus Life office phone number for young people who want to contact us during the week for counseling help.

Some can't wait that long. Art talked to a girl last night who didn't go on the air, but shared with Art her concern for her boy friend, Don, an escapee from a juvenile correctional center. He recently had been recaptured and was waiting to return to the facility from which he had run away. She was upset and asked if anyone could talk with Don and try to help him straighten out. Art calmed her down and said he would personally take the job!

Today he asked me to go with him to Juvenile Hall. We arranged to see Don. Art enjoyed keeping me in the dark as to just what this was all about until we were in the chaplain's office and Don was brought in. Only then did I learn of the phone call to the station.

In a direct way Art told Don his girlfriend genuinely cared for him, that escaping had been foolish, and that he ought to get his head together and make the best of his second chance back at the correction center because the next stop could be much worse. Don might have gotten that same advice from any number of people, but he was startled to hear it coming from someone his own age. And when he learned Art was facing a long prison sentence on a serious charge, Don sat up and took notice.

"Look, Don," Art advised, "there's a Bible rap group going at that place every Friday night and you ought to get in on it. Don't think you're chicken or something because you want to help yourself and learn about the Lord. If some of the guys give you a bad time for going to the rap session, so what? Those are the guys that end up spending a lot of time in places like that. Don't blow it, man. Make up your mind you're going to do the right thing and stay with it. I just wish I had the chance to go to a place like they're sending you instead of where they want to put me. Be thankful."

Don was amazed at the whole session but seemed to appreciate the counsel.

Our guest on the radio last night, by the way, was a senior official of the FBI, Charles Bates. He and Art met at the station, had a friendly visit, and got along well together.

January 10

Art was with me when I went to court today to testify for another young man I know. Our opponent, the deputy district attorney who cross-examined me, was not only a sharp young lawyer, but it was obvious from his questions that he really grasped what our ministry with young people is all about. He asked for the information he wanted, but he also paved the way for some clear-cut statements of our Christian principles. It was unusual.

After court he confirmed what I had thought; he is a sincere Christian with a great interest in young people. He met Art and was delighted to learn of Art's work with us. He asked Art and me to speak next week at the church youth group he sponsors (even though he lost the court case!).

"I hope the prosecutor on my case is like him," Art said as we left the courthouse.

I was almost late for my weekly Rotary Club luncheon, so I took Art with me instead of back to school.

"Do you think they'll know me?" Art asked as we arrived.

"I doubt it. You're dressed neatly and look like the all-American boy. Besides, people usually respond to what they expect, and the very last person in the world they'd expect to meet at a Rotary Club would be a bank robber!"

I was right. Art was given a warm welcome when I introduced him as "one of the high-school students in our program." Art leaned over and whispered, "That has to be the understatement of the year." He enjoyed a friendly visit with the men at the table—law enforcement officers, the mayor, and would you believe, a senior officer of Wells Fargo Bank! None gave a hint of knowing Art's history.

One man who should have recognized Art, but didn't, was the news director of KNTV, who edited and aired hundreds of feet of film on Art. He was very surprised after the meeting to discover that Art was *the* Art DePeralta. In fact, he was so surprised and impressed that he asked Art to come over to the station for a special news interview feature on what had happened since the robbery.

"So that's the establishment," Art commented as we left. "They're not at all like what I expected. They're a bunch of all-right guys."

"You know, Art," I replied, "they probably think the same about you!"

January 11

Art wanted me to try to help Jesse and Butch spiritually—although he didn't particularly want them to know he had suggested it. So today I drove to the San Francisco City Prison to see them.

Butch is nineteen, lanky, with an engaging smile. The strain of the case weighs heavily on him but doesn't quite erase the casual, easy-going manner that is more normally his. He was happy to meet me and eagerly accepted the *Reach Out* New Testament I brought him.

Through most of his teen years Butch has been on his own—literally. His parents turned him out; he spent many nights in a sleeping bag along the edges of creeks, unless he could spend a few days with a friend. Butch prided himself on his independence. It was a miserable way to live, wondering where he would sleep or get his next meal. Even now in custody he was more concerned about his two younger brothers and who might be influencing them than he was about his own predicament. His sister is a fine Christian woman, married, starting a family, and deeply concerned for all of her brothers.

It was while he was loose, unemployed, and hanging around the community not doing much that he met Jesse and Big Ben.

Some friends had once brought Butch to a Campus Life club meeting and he enjoyed it. I wish we had made contact with him and he had come back.

Jesse, twenty-three, I viewed with mixed emotions. Police reports indicated him to be a violent young man, ready to kill the hostages and shoot it out with the police. He gave me no such impression—but then so much had happened to him since the robbery.

At the time of the chase and shoot-out, he had been critically wounded by the shot in the head fired through the car window by the police marksman. The .357 Magnum bullet went through his skull over the eye, down through his throat and lodged in his neck where it still was. He had lost a huge amount of blood and police on the scene were convinced Jesse was either dead or would be by the time he reached the hospital.

But as he sat talking with me, his mental faculties appeared intact. He had recovered in the San Quentin Prison Hospital and had then been sent to the federal jail tank in San Francisco. He had lost the sight of one eye; the other one had not been good for some time. He had headaches; he'd lost the sense of smell and had an indentation over his eye where the bullet had gone in. It was amazing he was alive at all, able to walk, talk, think, and have a reasonably good memory.

"I served my tour in the Army in Vietnam. When I got home, I couldn't find a job, you know, anything steady. This added to the problems with my wife and that made me all the more on edge. I started drinking heavy."

Nothing seemed to have gone right for Jesse. That pattern didn't improve when he met Ben, Sr. and his friends.

Today Jesse seemed friendly enough. But I'm far from knowing everything about him.

January 12

Just what kind of a young man is it who makes headlines in a major, violent crime then, shortly after, is back in the community awaiting trial, going to school, trying to rebuild his life? It's a question I'm often asked.

If all there was to Art was what the news stories said then we'd be dealing with an unfeeling, cold, cruel individual. But Art is not that. He has strong feelings, so strong he often has to work hard to cover them up, especially around his old crowd where he has to maintain a certain image of the tough guy who doesn't care. Art can play that role and create that impression, but only for awhile.

He can order his younger brothers around like they were his slaves, but pity the outsider who would give any of his family a bad time when Art is nearby. He can have an argument with a girl friend and tell her he doesn't care about her and to "get lost," then go out a short time later and buy her flowers which he has delivered with a note of apology. Or he will lie awake at night trying to find the right way to say, "I'm sorry."

Like many nondelinquent youngsters, Art doesn't always appreciate going to school. Today marked the end of a week in which he had been to school five full days, a record for him. He didn't seem too overjoyed at the accomplishment.

With most adults he is unfailingly polite, which explains why a girlfriend's parents, who might not appreciate their daughter associating with a headline-making criminal, are almost invariably disarmed by Art. He is neat, relaxed, intelligent, well-spoken and parents of his friends cannot seem to link him in their minds to a major offense. Thus he enjoys a good deal of social acceptance.

Art is not the sociopath who has no genuine feelings for others. Far from being alienated, Art reaches out for friendship and approval. He wants desperately to be liked. But it is not surprising that when he finds a warmth in other people he often hesitates to be totally open for fear of being rejected again.

It is hard to imagine a boy who hurt his family, and especially his mother, more than Art did. But there is a deep and obvious attachment between Art and his mother.

Though he can be very articulate Art often has difficulty putting his true feelings into words, so he will write them in notes. Or he will find a way to show appreciation by a thoughtful kindness or a favor. If such an act is noticed he will shrug it off saying, "I didn't mean anything by it."

On the other hand, he can be rough and insensitive, even at play. He does not like to see people hurt, excluding, unfortunately, days like the one he robbed the bank. He will come to someone's aid, give generously of his time and ability when asked, and when thanked usually denies he had much to do with it. He is an expert mechanic skilled at repairing both cars and appliances and will gladly give hours to working on such things with no thought of reward.

Then he can turn around and be very greedy, grasping and selfish, wanting his own way. And he can create logical patterns of argumentation that leave his desires the only sensible course of action, no matter how another person viewed the situation at first.

He can be an ardent follower of the Lord one minute, and the next show an attitude much more akin to the devil!

He wants to be an individual, loved, noticed, appreciated. He knows how badly he has been abused and manipulated by adults he trusted, and he shows his resentment by sometimes doing the same thing to others.

But through it all there's a bright spot: Art wants to be a man doing the right thing. Rebuke him and he'll get angry, but he will later admit you were right and come back for more.

Give him instructions or set limits, and he'll test those limits to the hilt and yell loudly about his independence and doing his own thing, but he won't cross the line once he knows it has been drawn, that it is right, and there is no compromise to be won.

The truth is, most young people in his situation would have given up a long time ago. People trying to help such kids often are told to forget it once the youth feels crowded. Not so with Art.

His "friends" keep saying he'll run away and skip bail. Such talk angers Art.

"That's ridiculous," he says. "Where could I go that the authorities wouldn't find me? No place. Then my folks would lose everything. I couldn't do that to them no matter what I face. Besides, I gave my word I'd stay and that is exactly what I am going to do."

As I was writing these pages Art came in and looked them over carefully, then commented, "That's quite an evaluation of me you've written. I could argue about some of it, but it hits things pretty well." Then he thought some more and added, "I'll probably be a lot different when I'm not facing court, a trial and going to prison."

Art tries to hide his feelings and concern but it is obvious the tension of all the events is very much on his mind and bothers him deeply.

I agreed with him about the current tensions affecting his thinking and conduct, then I added, "You know, Art, the more you learn about Christ's power and control in your life, and the more you trust Him and let Him guide you, the sooner you will mature into the man you want to be and God wants you to be."

I shared with him two key verses from 1 Peter 4: "Dear friends, don't be bewildered or surprised when you go through the fiery trials ahead, for this is no strange, unusual thing that is happening to you. Instead, be really glad—because these trials will make you partners with Christ in His suffering, and afterwards you will have the wonderful joy of sharing His glory in that coming day when it will be displayed" (verses 12, 13).

We talked about Art's future, completing his education, getting married, settling down, raising a family—all things very much on his mind.

"I know I've got to be ready, in every way, for responsibilities like that," he said, "and the Lord is going to have to be the One to do it in my life.

"Look," he concluded, "you keep encouraging me to grow as a Christian and do what is right. There are times I hate you for it, but don't give up. Don't quit. Okay?"

Give up on Art? Not a chance.

The future is too bright.

January 13

Santa Clara County has a juvenile facility near San Jose, the William F. James Ranch at Morgan Hill.

The ranch gives the appearance of being a private school, and a good one at that. There are no locks, fences or uniformed guards. There's a good school program, more than adequate living and recreational facilities, a generally relaxed atmosphere, and a good counseling program for both the boy and his family. A work program, home visits, and the ministry of Campus Life are all added features. The program is highly successful.

Art should have been sent to the ranch—in fact, he almost was, twenty days before the bank robbery. Instead, he got his "one more chance." Tonight he was at the ranch with Mr. Ubhaus to take part in a program for the eighty boys. Each Friday evening, Dan and I lead what is basically an informal Campus Life discussion built around applying the Lord's message to their needs. Tonight's was a special presentation program for the entire group.

After the music of *Gabriel*, the same musical group as featured at the "Living End," Art was to give a short talk. He had some friends in the group. John Hafner, who had visited him at Juvenile Hall, was there, and Don, the fellow Art had talked to at the request of his girl friend, plus a number of guys Art knew from the streets.

Art sat down on the edge of the stage, the house dark, overhead lights on him, a microphone in his hand. It was a very casual approach.

"Guys, I'm not here to tell you how to live or solve all your problems for you. I've got a big enough job working things out in my own life. Most of you know what I did, and I didn't come out here to brag about some big job I pulled. I'll tell you what happened, mainly so you can see how things can build to far more trouble than a guy ever planned on."

Slowly and quietly, with hardly a whisper in the crowd to distract, Art told of the events in his life that led up to November 30. He talked about not listening to his folks, not caring about school, the crowd he ran with, the life they led, and the result.

"Now here I am, the same age as you guys, and yet facing something far bigger and worse than any of you. You might ask why do I care about my future at all, why do I give a damn? Well, I'll tell you. Because I know how much my family really loves me. I pretty much took them for granted until the day they put everything they had ever worked for on the line so I could get out of custody after I'd really hurt them. That was enough to leave me concerned but not enough to put me together again right.

"That's where the Lord comes in. If a guy gets a new car and something is wrong with it he can't fix himself, then he doesn't just take it to some jerk mechanic in the neighborhood to get it running. He takes it back to the company that made it and tells them to fix it.

"It's the same in life. When you can't straighten things out yourself and your friends have as many problems as you do, where do you turn? How about going back to the Guy who made you, God? He did the job right in the first place. You blew it, and He seems to be the best One to set things right. At least that's how I figure it, and on December 6 I got a rebirth, a rebuilding job on a badly out-of-tune life.

"And I got it from a great Mechanic, the Lord. I'd never had much to do with Him before. I had sort of suggested He and I just stay out of each other's way. Then, in Juvenile Hall, I was in a position where I had to find someone or something or I was all through.

"The books about Nicky Cruz showed me pretty clearly how God changed a very mixed-up guy. Some of the things I read in *The Way* told how Christ cared enough to give His life for me, then busted out of the grave to prove everything He claimed was true. He seemed like a good place, the only place, to start with my problem.

"Gordy spoke at a church the other day and he was telling the kids about the people who found Jesus when he was born. The busy crowd at the party in the Bethlehem Holiday Inn didn't even know what was going on in the stable out back. Some wise men found Jesus, though, and so did some shepherds. Two kinds of people got to the Lord: wise men smart enough to know they didn't know everything, and simple people who went looking.

"I guess the same kind of people still find Him today. I hope you're one of them. Thank you."

The applause was long and loud. The boys crowded around Art to wish him well and thank him for coming. Several asked to talk personally with Dan and me about what Art had said.

January 18

Both Art and Ben, Jr. seemed unusually depressed today, very much on edge. They weren't too eager to talk about what was bugging them. Finally Art told me.

"Ben, Jr. got a letter yesterday. It was delivered to his home, not mailed. It's pretty upsetting." Now that I knew about the letter, it still took awhile to learn its contents.

The letter was not signed, but the authorship could be narrowed down to several people, all of whom were close to what was happening. Art finally read some of the lines.

"You can take it lightly or you can take it serious as you should. Because this is deadly serious, believe it or not. I know you'll take Art the Rat's side . . . but I would advise you to think for yourself. Get some names and addresses of people that don't like Art, like people he has beat up on . . . or better yet give him a fix of rat poison when he gets real loaded. If you can convince Art to say to the FBI that the reason he change (*sic*) his mind . . . is because he received a phone call telling him that if he didn't change his testimony . . . that his mother and family were going to get kill (*sic*)."

That was only part of it.

Art's not particularly worried about himself, but he is greatly concerned over anyone else getting hurt.

We'll simply have to be on guard.

In the meantime, I showed him a verse in the Bible: "When a man is trying to please God, God makes even his worst enemies to be at peace with him" (Proverbs 16:7).

January 19

"I don't feel like going to school today," Art announced as Dan went to give him a ride across town to classes.

"Why?"

"It's a drag. I just get tired of it." Art's eyes narrowed. "You can't make me go."

"Probably not," Dan replied. "But you don't want to put me in the place of having to tell the magistrate you won't do what you agreed to do when you got out, do you? He just might not like that."

"You mean you'd turn me in?" Art asked.

"Of course not," Dan replied, "because it won't be necessary. Not when you're in school."

If looks could kill, Dan would have been on his way to the morgue at that very minute.

Art may just have been in a bad mood. He likes his new school, and they like him.

Art went to school, but it cost Dan two large bottles of 7-Up to get him to the classroom. It's a good thing 7-Up isn't addicting or Art would really be hooked.

While Art was heading for his classes I had a conference with his county juvenile probation officer, who had supervised him for over a year.

"Art's a really intelligent kid," the officer told me, "and it's too bad his interest and ability has never been really challenged by something worthwhile.

"He has talked and manipulated his way out of situations that would finish off the average kid. He can be pleasant and smooth, and the next minute very cold. I'm going to go slow in believing he's really changed and turned to God. I can't help it; I've been through too much with him. I hope it's genuine, and if it is, you've got an outstanding young man on your hands. I'll be watching.

"Don't get me wrong. I'm not against the kid. He's very likable and much more open in our talks since the bank robbery and his arrest. I really hope he makes it. We sure didn't reach him here."

When Dan told me about having to coax him to school, it only reinforced what the probation officer had said. Change has to be proved to be believed. Art is changing from a background of complete indifference to responsibility and is at the same time facing all the frustrations and pressures of pending court actions and likely imprisonment. He has his low moments, his discouragements, and his failures. Some problems come not because he doesn't care, but because he wants to be too strong too fast. Other difficulties come as he contrasts what he learns from his Christian friends with the habits and attitudes of his old life. A victory on the good side is impossible without the strength of God's Word and the power of the Spirit, and both are new and unfamiliar to Art.

The situation is a delicate one for Dan, me and all of our Campus Life staff. Naturally we want to see Art grow in his faith and make the right decisions. But we dare not push him; Art balks when he's pressured.

Working with Art is teaching me a lot about patience.

I'm also facing something else. Standards are to build my life, but they are not a gauge to measure anyone else, including Art. I can offer counsel and suggestions; I've earned that right. But there the imposition of my desires must stop and the Lord must take over. If Art does things I don't like or approve of, that's too bad for me. If I really accept him, as the Lord wants me to, the acceptance must not be conditional.

I can't say, even in my own mind, "Art, I like you but you'll have to stop...." I've got to accept him as he is. With his temper and habits and streaks of poor attitude, that isn't easy.

Not long ago a friend handed me a card that might well apply to Art: "Please be patient. God isn't through working on me yet."

January 20

Of all the audiences Art might meet, today was undoubtedly his greatest test. It was like Daniel volunteering for the lions' den when he agreed to speak at a law enforcement conference attended by police officers from all over the state. He wasn't sure he should even accept the invitation, but finally decided he would.

The detective sergeant who introduced him certainly captured the interest of the group:

"Six weeks ago I was in the lead car of thirty vehicles pursuing the young man you are about to meet. The pace was fast and I had to dodge the bullets being fired at my car from his. That day I very much wanted to capture or kill him and I believe he would have been delighted to see me dead. Today we have met and talked as friends who, by the way, share a common commitment of personal faith in the Lord. It would appear that he is a changed man. I hope that is true and if it is, I wish him well in the future. I certainly never want to meet him again with a loaded gun ready for action in either of our hands. I hope you find talking with him as enjoyable an experience as I did today."

Then Art spoke. He was quiet, careful, weighing every word, aware of the basic hostility and skepticism in the audience. But he was honest about himself, his mistakes, how he had gotten into trouble and what had happened since. The group warmed considerably, much to their own surprise.

When it came time for questions, an obvious one was asked.

"How did the officers treat you at the time of your arrest?"

"They were rough at first, grabbing me as I surrendered, pulling my hair and throwing me to the ground. But they almost had to be that way. They didn't know if I had other weapons, would be violent or what. Besides, I think the officers were very tense after the long chase, just as I was. But once they searched me and checked carefully for weapons, they relaxed. From that point on, I was treated well by all the officers. The FBI men have always been fair and proper in their handling and interviews."

Then the questioning took an unexpected turn. Perhaps as the police officers looked at the young man before them, dressed neatly and talking politely, they got the uneasy feeling that one of their own sons might be up front. They mentally took off their badges and began to react as people, and more particularly as parents. They wanted to know what could have been done in Art's home, or theirs, to prevent this kind of tragedy. They asked about family communication, discipline, cooperation, values. Art made no claim at being an expert, but he responded as best he could with ideas and suggestions.

"Always let your children know you love them. Let them come home and feel free to talk with you about anything on their mind. You don't have to take their side when they are wrong against the school or the police," (laughter) "but at least listen to them. You don't help a kid when you let him have his own way all the time. You show real love when you set some reasonable and fair limits. Young people want that and expect it."

He received a long and spontaneous ovation when he was through.

January 25

Art shared at another Campus Life club meeting tonight, this one for Westmont High School students. The clubs are casual, in the informal setting of a home, with plenty of fun, a serious discussion and a wrap-up by a staff member grounded in his faith who loves, and can relate to, the high-school crowd.

Appearing very much like another kid in the group, Art sat on a stool and told the group how accepting the Lord had given him some hope for the future when his life had been so wrong and tragically mixed up. They listened.

After the meeting students filled out reaction cards. Here is a sampling:

"I haven't really accepted there being a God. It sounds interesting and I think I'll look into it."

"I think now the point about God is getting across."

"The speaker was someone who had the credentials to make you listen and think."

"I got the feeling he meant every word he said."

"Tonight was really good and you got the point across that God is the one to turn to if you're in trouble or not."

"It was good to have Art come and share his experience with us. I kind of think a couple of people didn't like it, but the message was put out to accept or reject."

"The meeting had a lot of value showing me what I really needed most."

Unanimously good comments? No. "Why do we need a bank robber to come here and talk about God? If he knew about God and cared about anybody else he wouldn't be in all that trouble. How do we know this isn't just something he's saying? This Christ trip doesn't do anything for people. I'm still an atheist."

But on the other hand, "Each meeting I've learned more, and each meeting I've come closer to God, but this meeting was the best when Art was talking. I could really relate to him and what he was saying."

"This meeting helped me . . . I will be praying for the young man."

January 26

Nicky Cruz and Billy Graham's close associate, T. W. Wilson, have both written Art personal letters of encouragement. They enclosed some good material that will be a real boost in Art's understanding his new life as a Christian.

Art picked up copies of *The Way* for his girl friend, another friend of hers, Ben, Jr., and his fiancee, RoseAnn. They've all been looking at the copies Art and his brothers have, and wanted their own. So Art decided to do some missionary work among his closest friends.

January 30

Art and his girl friend, along with Ben, Jr. and RoseAnn, came over to my apartment and we had some Bible study together. It's wonderful to see their sincerity and desire to learn; we really didn't worry too much about the time.

At the conclusion I said to Art, "As long as it's late, take my car home; then pick me up in the morning. From there I'll drop you off at school." Agreed.

January 31

Bright and very early, Art called this morning. "Did I wake you up?" he asked. (I was tempted to say, "No, you didn't wake me up. I had to get up to answer the phone anyway." But I didn't this time.)

"You won't believe this, Gordy," Art continued, "but your nice new car and I have been in an accident."

He was right. I didn't believe it. Art often called and began by telling me he was in the hospital, in jail again, or had suffered some other dire fate. He was always joking.

Unfortunately, today he wasn't. He had gone into a skid on a turn where gravel had spilled on a wet road. The car had crashed into a pole. The front end of the car was badly smashed, the passengers only shaken up. The pole survived well.

One of the staff men picked me up and drove me to the scene where we found Art, very dismayed. I reserved my reaction until I talked to the investigating officer. I thought to myself, *Art, this is all you need to seal your doom with the police!*

"I think he was driving too fast for conditions," the officer said, "but not so fast as to conclude he was speeding or to justify giving him a ticket."

That was it. They took my car away to be repaired and I was left the chore of explaining to my insurance agent how a bank robber wrecked my car.

Art seemed genuinely sorry about the accident. There was no point in getting mad at him;

it would solve nothing, and he is a good driver most of the time.

(There was one consolation. He went to school today without argument.)

February 4

Yesterday was Art's birthday. He had a good day with his girl friend. Today, after church and dinner, he and I went for a ride and a long talk.

"There are a lot of things about me you don't know. Many of your friends think I'm a nice kid who accidentally got into some big trouble that I was talked into. That isn't true. I want you to know about me, all I've done. Then you'll never be surprised if some guy comes up and says, 'Art did this job' or 'Art did that.'

"My dad was a hard-working guy, a Filipino. He and my mom split up when I was three months old. I lived with both of them at various times. Later my mother remarried and my stepfather, as you know, is hard-working, too. He's a lot stricter than my real father.

"I first cut school in the second grade; it was a religion class as I remember. I started shoplifting in about the fourth grade. If I couldn't get the money for something I wanted, I just took it.

"When I was young my dad and I did a lot of things together, especially hunting. I had my own high-powered pellet gun when I was eight, and I knew how to use it. When I was ten, I had my first .22 rifle, and when I was eleven I got my first six-point deer.

"From as far back as I could remember I liked engines and cars as well as motorcycles. I had my first Honda 50 when I was ten.

"My hunting career came to a halt when I accidentally shot a horse. My dad took away my rifle and said, 'I don't want to see you with a gun again until you're eighteen.'

"When I was twelve we lived on a ranch out

in the country. I got used to driving a lot. I liked school back then and was doing well.

"My cousin Tom and I were buddies. His dad, my Uncle Max, was a merchant seaman, and when he'd come home from a trip of three or four months, he'd bring us radios or other things from places like Hong Kong or the Philippines or Japan.

"My shoplifting kept up. Once I got caught and the manager of the store put me in a storeroom while he went to call the cops. I managed to open a window and crawl out before he got back.

"I worked around the farm with Tom and my buddies. We'd work hard, then relax at the end of the day with some of the wildest tomato wars you ever saw.

"Then, when I was fourteen, my dad remarried. I didn't know about it until it was done. Not only did that hurt me, but my new stepmother made it very clear that I was in the way and she really didn't want me around. About then my dad retired and things were pretty rough for him so I split and came to stay with my mother.

"I wasn't used to the limits and controls she and my stepfather had long established for my younger brothers and sister. The scene was a little tense.

"I enrolled in high school, but wasn't what you'd call the most studious guy. I got into a fight with another kid one day at school. It was the wrestling coach who caught us and broke it up. 'I'll make a deal with you, kid,' he said. 'I won't turn you in if you'll join my squad.' So that's how I started wrestling. In the tenth grade, I wrestled at a hundred eighteen pounds with the varsity team and was undefeated.

"In my spare time I loved to work on cars

and I got to where I could fix them good.

"But except for wrestling, I just wasn't that interested in school. The subject material was stuff I didn't see any use in knowing. Many of the teachers cared only about getting through the book and what grade you got, not how much you learned. It was getting to be a real drag.

"So I quit and joined the Army. I really liked that. Boot camp is no picnic, but I was doing okay until they found out I was sixteen and not old enough to be there. I was soon back out on the streets again and less ready for school than before.

"I was often out smoking grass, and eventually tried most of the things like reds, whites, coke (cocaine), but never the hard stuff. None of that needle stuff for me.

"One night I got busted when I was out with this girl I really liked. They got us for possession of marijuana. Nothing much came of the deal but her parents were furious, separated us and sent her away.

"I kept messing around. One night a bunch of us guys got a girl and we shared her so we each got a piece of the action. She told her mom, and the cops were out looking for me, so I split for awhile.

"When I was jamming around I saw there was some money to be made dealing dope, so I got into that and learned how much really big money there is in that stuff.

"The first armed robbery I ever did was at a small photo store in a parking lot. It was easy, quick, and I had a few hundred bucks.

"About then I started going over to Big Ben's, mainly to get loaded. I had met Butch and Jesse when they were hanging around my school seeing some chicks they knew, and now they were over at Big Ben's. We really had a good time. We'd often play around with guns and practice up on our shooting. We even had our own version of cowboy games. I played Jesse James.

"But I was also out doing the real thing. Sometimes with Butch and Jesse or with other guys.

"There was one store we ripped off, I remember well. My partner had a pistol and I had a knife. We wore beanies well down over our faces and waited until the customers left. Then we went in. This old guy was on duty and we tied him up, gagged him, took all the cash and left. It was smooth.

"Big Ben was like a father to us in many ways. We called him the Godfather. He's in a wheelchair, but don't let that kid you; he's tough. He's been in some big prisons, and he's in that chair because he got shot by the cops down south and they left him to die. But Ben was too tough and pulled through.

"He'd help us with our jobs. Tell us how to do it, see we had the guns. We always cut him in for an equal share, plus he got all the change.

"He was good at it, too. He'd take the little kids out riding and have a couple of guys hiding in the trunk. They'd stop, the guys would get out of the trunk, run into a store, pull their heist, then get back in the trunk and Big Ben would drive off. Who would suspect a crippled guy with some kids in the front seat of pulling a job? Nobody ever looked in the trunk for my partners.

"We had a chance to really score one night on a junkie. These guys make lots of bread and are good to rip off. They ain't about to call the cops.

"At this one guy's pad, my partner and I came up with a gun, smashed in the door, threw the surprised guy up against the wall and demanded his cash. My partner went looking for the guy's stash and the guy started getting rowdy with me. When he tried to jump me, I shot him in the leg. We got our money—eight Gs—and left. The guy didn't get any revenge. A few weeks later, the cops shot and killed him during a bust.

"It was after this the banking business came up. My partners hit a bank and got eighteen thousand dollars. That's not bad for a few minutes' work. And they got away clean. It beat some of the jobs I was doing with them. We'd get a few hundred bucks sometimes, but I remember once we held up a guy, took all that risk, and got eighteen dollars. It was a lousy deal.

"So when the guys asked if I wanted in on the job we did in November at the bank, I said sure. They figured we'd each get at least twenty-five thousand dollars. That would get me a sharp short (car), some spending money, and even pay for college.

"No one talked me into it. I wouldn't have gone in on the job if I hadn't wanted to. And I had plenty of preparation for it ahead of time.

"That's the kind of person I've been. Sure, I've been mean. I'm afraid to trust people. My father promised me a lot of things, like, he'd buy me a car and other stuff. When he got married again, he just dropped everything he told me. I trusted other people and they burned me. I thought Big Ben would stick with me no matter what.

He always said we'd stick together. When I really needed him, he was nowhere around. I could have died inside that bank for all he cared.

"Now you're saying you're my friend and, more important, I can really trust the Lord. He won't let me down. If that's true, He'll be the first one who ever came through."

"Well, the Lord hasn't done badly by you so far, has He?" I asked.

"No, He hasn't," Art acknowledged.

Art was pretty tired from our long talk. He had told me everything he thought important about his past and his associates. It was information he had not shared with anyone else.

February 5

Art was in court again, this time with a motion to sever his trial from that of the other three accused. The government raised no objections and the motion was granted.

Art is set to start classes at the community college tomorrow. He's also been out looking for work but, aside from the fact that part-time jobs are scarce, he is pretty well-known from all the press and television coverage. It hasn't helped. Then he has to have time off for court appearances. He may just have to pass up working for awhile.

February 7

Art came over to my apartment for the evening with Ben, Jr. and RoseAnn. The two had been digging into *The Way* and had some questions Art wasn't yet ready to handle.

"You know, Gordy, I've never had much to do with the Bible," Ben, Jr. said after a while. "But I'm with Art every day and I've seen him trying to do things right now; I've seen some real changes."

"At my job," RoseAnn added, "there's a girl who really knows the Lord, and she's been talking with me about Him. Then I've been doing some reading. It just seems like a great new way of living."

"That it is, and much more," I replied, and together we sat and shared the invitation God makes for us to receive His Son and start a new life that goes on forever.

Before the evening was over, Art's two closest friends had met the Lord.

February 12

Today we went to the studios of the Family Radio Network to record an interview to be heard on Christian FM stations across the country. In a simple, factual way Art told the interviewer what had happened, about accepting Christ, and the difference such a commitment can make.

"I don't enjoy reliving a terrible experience or talking about it," he told the audience, "but if talking will help some young people to change their ways, or parents to care, or anybody to find the Lord, then I'll do it. If I had known the Lord I wouldn't be in the jam I'm in now."

February 20

Today as Art and I went to speak at a high school, we invited John Hafner to join us. He made a welcome addition.

If you want a magazine cover photo of the clean-cut, all-American boy, take a picture of John. Well-built, nice looking, well-dressed, pleasant, very intelligent, he looks like the boy you'd want your sister to date. But looks can be deceiving.

John had to contend with an alcohol problem in his home that split apart his parents. Alateen, the counseling program for young people who have alcoholic parents, was a good help, but in this case, not quite enough.

Living with his mother, John was soon beyond her control. He had some ambitions and he wasn't about to go without the things he wanted just because the family financial security had been shattered by liquor. For John it was a fairly easy jump from "I want something" to "I need it" to "I don't care how I get it."

That's when he started stealing.

One day a buddy shared some interesting news. There was a family in the neighborhood that kept a large envelope of cash on hand, and it would be easy to break in and rip them off.

John was game. He and the buddy went over to the house a few nights later, entered through the garage, and surprised a young boy, the only one home. John held a pellet gun to his head. Then they took him upstairs and tied him to a bed so they could ransack the house looking for the money envelope. It was nowhere to be found.

Suddenly John heard the lady of the house drive in. He went down to the kitchen to intercept her. The woman was not alone; her young niece was with her. The two came in from the garage to face John and his gun.

"Actually," John commented, "I was getting more scared by the minute. By the time these two people came in I was shaking in my boots. If she had reached over and taken the gun out of my hand, it would have been all over there and then. She could have had the weapon."

Perhaps, but few people are about to take that risk. Instead, they were ordered upstairs, shoved into a closet, and blocked in with a heavy chest of drawers.

Then John and his partner continued to ransack the house, loading everything valuable into the family Cadillac. Finally they left to deliver their merchandise to the "fence" who had arranged earlier to take the goods off their hands, left the car, and went home.

John was asleep several hours later when the police came to arrest him. The niece had recognized John's partner.

He went to the state institution, John himself to the James Ranch.

At the ranch, John settled outwardly into the program. But inside he was a bundle of confused emotions, values and goals, and both he and his counselor knew it.

He was looking for some answers about himself and his future. His counselor helped him a good deal; so did the group meetings. Then one night his counselor suggested he talk with Dan and me.

That's how I happened to meet a young man who said bluntly, "I've got a lot of questions and problems to look into, and I've been told you've got some answers."

I was more than a little taken back and responded, "I hate to disappoint you. But I have a big enough job working out things in my own life without taking on your hang-ups. But I do know Someone who can make a tremendous difference in how you're living if you get to know Him."

We went through plenty of questions for several weeks before John reached his conclusion. "I don't know everything there is to know about God and His plan, but I guess I'll never know anything about it if I don't start somewhere. If the Lord can forgive me and change my life, I'm ready to let Him." That night John met Christ.

He had his battles with consistency and following through. If there was an easy way around responsibility, John would find it. But neither his counselor nor I would let him settle for that. Step-by-step John learned to get up after disappointments, be honest with himself, and put out his best effort, not just get by.

He grew in his faith as well. He responded to our urgings that he systematically spend time in God's Word. The theory is that a person becomes like the crowd he runs with. By spending a lot of time with Jesus Christ, we become more like Him. For John especially, that was bound to be an improvement.

John developed into a positive leader and influence among his peers at the ranch. He also joined us in many community programs sharing his background, experiences, talking about the ranch as well as his plans for the future.

John has been home for some time now. He called on the family he robbed to apologize for what he'd done to them. He's done well in his studies and is active in Campus Life. He was even elected class president.

When we wanted someone of similar experience to give Art encouragement while he was still in custody, John was the one we chose.

John always looked like a fine young man.

Now he is.

March 3

When I returned today from our YFC/Campus Life staff conference in Portland, I read some sad news involving teen-agers.

Yesterday some high-school students had been out driving around in one boy's car over the noon hour. The roads were wet and slippery, and they had some malt liquor.

In the excitement, one young passenger had turned to Chris, the driver, and said, "Let's see if you can fishtail it." The car quickly leaped ahead, spun out of control and crashed into a couple of trees, finally coming to rest against a house. The boy in the front passenger seat died, two passengers had broken limbs and internal injuries. Chris was hardly hurt and, after a checkup at the county medical center, was booked into Juvenile Hall on manslaughter charges.

Art was with me when I stopped in at the hall this morning. We learned that Chris was tremendously distraught over the tragedy, had eaten barely anything and had said practically nothing. The staff was concerned about him.

I brought the young man into the chaplain's office. It was Art who kindly shared with Chris, and beyond lifting his spirits, offered some genuine encouragement.

"Chris, not too long ago I sat for nearly three weeks in that same receiving room you're now in. I know how discouraging it can get. I know what it means to feel lonely, scared and bitterly ashamed for what you've done ... to face your parents and people you've hurt. I was arrested for something far different than what got you here, but the feelings may be close to the same. I'm home now and I never thought I would be. I've got the pressures of court actions coming, people looking down on me, even hating me for what I did. You may get some of the same.

"I wouldn't have made it at all, or even wanted to, if it hadn't been for something that happened to me in this office on December 6. That day I looked at the mess my life was in, knew I couldn't begin to straighten it out, and asked the Lord to come into my life. There were no big claps of thunder in the sky, but something happened inside me and it's made a big difference in so many things. My attitude, feelings, goals all are changed and I'm glad. I've still got plenty of problems and faults but some things are starting to really come together."

I couldn't have asked for a better introduction to my sharing the news of God's love with Chris and leaving him a *Reach Out* plus some books to read.

March 8

The only person who looks less like a drug dealer than Andy Freedman is the narc who busted him. He surprises people and that's one reason Andy is such a good speaker at parents' meetings, and why Art and I had Andy join us tonight.

Andy is a pleasant, neat young man, small for his age. But what he lacks in physical size he more than makes up for with his forceful personality and enthusiasm. You come away from meeting him convinced here is a young man with a great future who really has his head together. And you are right.

It wasn't always that way.

Andy took every advantage of the situation when his parents divorced; it was kind of good, in his terms, to play one against the other. He was almost guaranteed having his own way. But such power also left him quite insecure and frustrated.

In junior high school when some of his buddies were smoking bush, Andy was curious enough to join them, and unhappy enough to find the experience a welcome relief from his tedious everyday routine.

There are many willing to argue at the drop of a joint that marijuana doesn't act as the first rung up a ladder leading to the use of drugs. Interestingly, I've never heard that argument from anybody who is heavily into the drug scene. More often it comes from young experimenters or intellectuals seeking to justify its use. Certainly it would be absurd to say everyone who uses grass will end up heavily into the drug culture, but it's even more ridiculous to say that some users won't.

It's also easy to get the issue sidetracked into questions such as marijuana vs. alcohol. The truth is neither of them do much good. Or you can muddy the waters further and argue that some of the penalties for marijuana use are too severe, which they may very well be.

The main problem is still this: There's only one reason to smoke grass and that is to get stoned, loaded, high or whatever term you choose. In short, it's a waste. And it can be worse with the young and immature who soon may find there are bigger and more potent experiences in the drug culture for those who care to follow.

Andy found the drug route quite appealing to his personal desires, and also fairly profitable as he made the short step from user to small-time dealer. Grass, acid and reds were his line and business was brisk among his peers at school.

One customer, who looked even younger than Andy, made a few buys, then introduced Andy to an older friend who wanted more drugs. Both of Andy's newly-found customers turned out to be narcs, and Andy was soon popped and on his way to the James Ranch.

He did well in the program there, getting his head cleared up, benefiting much from counseling, and catching up on his school work. The Campus Life visits to the ranch Friday night meant little to Andy; he was Jewish, and he figured he could do very nicely without the Christians.

But one of his counselee brothers, a young man who formerly had many problems but at the time was very much on the right track, began to share with Andy the differences Jesus could make in a life. Andy was sufficiently interested to ask for a *Reach Out* and start digging into it.

Then he began to come to the meetings and started asking questions. He was really getting involved—and all on his own. One night several months later came the request: "I've been thinking about this for a long time. I don't want to go back on drugs when I get out, but I do need something to fill the void in my life. And I've seen what Jesus can do in some of the guys here and I want to know Him. Will you help me?"

Gladly. And that's how Andy met the Lord. That's what he shared with the people tonight. He's not any less Jewish, he wanted them to know, he's added on a faith in Christ and his life is now more complete. He's been home for a number of months, working and going to school and sharing his faith every chance he gets. Art and he had a busy evening answering questions about their separate backgrounds and experiences.

It was Andy who had the last word. "You Christians ought to appreciate us Jews. Your whole thing got started with One of us."

He's right.

March 15

Chris has been released pending a court hearing on the manslaughter charge. Art and I spent some time with Chris today. Joe Silva is his attorney, so the court matters are in good hands.

"Remember what you guys talked to me about last week in the hall?" Chris asked, picking up *Reach Out*. "After you left I went back to my room in receiving and did a lot of thinking. I'm not much on praying but I asked God to come into my life and help me straighten out some things I can't do alone. I still don't know all about what happened but I've been learning, and I like it."

You don't always get quick results, but when you do, it's nice.

March 25

For the past three days, we've been in Bakersfield with fifteen hundred high-school students from all over California for the annual Campus Life Faith Festival.

Art, his girl friend and two of his brothers all attended. For them, as with many others, the seminar on sex, dating and marriage was one session they made sure to attend.

Afterwards, Art commented, "What the Bible says about love can get pretty heavy." He was referring to 1 Corinthians 13—"Love is very patient and kind, never jealous... selfish or rude. Love does not demand its own way. It is not irritable or touchy."

It's not surprising the Christian view of giving, not taking, was new to Art. Everything his crowd wanted they took. Why not treat a girl the same way?

Art was not the only one at the conference having problems of biblical concepts vs. contemporary society. Only he may have been a little more honest about it than some.

Between sessions, Art used some of his free time to share his experiences with the young people at the local Juvenile Hall, a program arranged as part of YFC's Youth Guidance ministry.

When they first saw Art, the kids in the hall thought he was a new boy just admitted, but they soon were giving rapt attention as Art told of his problems, his struggles and the faith giving him the strength to go on.

"Hey, man," one fellow asked, "are you really digging this Jesus trip?"

"It's no trip—it's a way of life," Art replied.

"And yes, I'm digging it. If it weren't for the Lord, I'd have given up all hope, maybe killed myself, or at least run as far and as fast as I could when I got out. You can count on one thing. If the Lord weren't very much in my life, I sure wouldn't be here now talking to you. I'd be long gone from this part of the world."

March 28

Art, Mr. Ubhaus, and I had a long conversation today to go over some important aspects of the coming court actions. There is little doubt in Art's mind that he will enter a guilty plea at the appropriate time. Being caught in the act of committing the crime, there's really little other sensible choice.

But the question now is what about testifying for the government at the trial of the other three? It appears Jesse and Butch will be convicted easily. But some additional testimony certainly could bolster the government's case against Ben, Sr.; and the U.S. attorney not only wants Art's statements given when he was arrested, but Art himself on the stand.

"If you testify, it should help you when your own case is heard—but there is certainly no deal being offered now for your testimony," Mr. Ubhaus told Art.

"I'm sure if I testify everyone will think the government bought me off in some way," Art commented, "and I don't want that. We all participated in the robbery and should be treated pretty much alike in the courts.

"I'm not out to get anybody, nor do I want to help anybody else get someone," Art added.

However there was another consideration and I raised it.

"Art, we're back to a basic issue of honesty again. If you're on a witness stand, it's not primarily to help someone or hurt somebody else. It's to tell the truth, and that's a duty everyone of us has. It's certainly our Christian responsibility."

"But if I do, nobody will believe I testified except to help myself get immunity or something else," Art insisted. "Gordy, you may look at this as an issue of doing the right thing because it is the right thing, but nobody else will see it that way. That just isn't the way it is."

There was one final factor, and Art himself presented it.

"We were supposed to be a family all together. Big Ben told us it was all for one and one for all. We would always look out for each other. Then at the bank, Butch cut out and Big Ben was nowhere around when we needed help."

Art drew a grim but true conclusion from his comments. "They left us in that bank alone to die."

He sat thinking quietly. No one said a word for several minutes.

Then he turned to his attorney. "I'll let you know what I decide."

April 8

Today was the first Sunday of the baseball season, with the Minnesota Twins in Oakland to play the A's. Art and I were the Twins' guests today for their morning chapel service. About half of the Twins were there; our host was pitching ace Jim Kaat.

Art shared with the team his background and experiences, the problems he was in, and his faith in Christ. Many of the players, young in their own faith, could readily identify with him. An old friend, Don Shinnick, a coach with the Oakland Raiders football team and a fine Christian, also joined us. It was a moving experience.

Naturally Art was impressed too. He met men who were familiar from the daily sports pages and whom he found to be down-to-earth guys with a real commitment to the Lord. He left with an autographed baseball, some new friends to remember, and a good boost in his life as a Christian.

On the way to meet the team, we stopped so Art could buy sunglasses. When he found the pair he liked, the clerk commented, "You ought to take those. They make you look like a federal agent!"

Art doubled over laughing. "Me, a fed? You have got to be kidding! If only you knew. I'll take them."

April 10

Unless you've sat in court for a while, you don't know how *unlike* Perry Mason and other TV dramas the real thing is. There aren't very many last-minute tearful confessions or emotional appeals to the jury. Even in a major criminal trial, much of the evidence is routine and boring except to the parties involved. But it's necessary to build great detail into the evidence since every defendant is presumed to be innocent until the prosecution proves his guilt "beyond a reasonable doubt and to a moral certainty."

In all federal felony trials and in the courts of most states, twelve jurors must be unanimous before a guilty verdict can be returned. The jury can acquit the defendant, again by a unanimous decision in most courts, or it can fail to agree, becoming a "hung jury," which usually results in a new trial being ordered.

But real trials are not without their suspense. It is hard to describe, but someone who is close to a case can often get a feeling of the impact the various witnesses are having individually and cumulatively. The climax, both legally and emotionally, comes as the verdict is finally rendered.

One feature of federal court sessions makes jury selection move much more rapidly than in many state trials. The U.S. federal judge questions the jurors rather than the attorneys. The attorneys on both sides, however, may still excuse jurors for valid cause, request specific questions to be asked of jurors, and eliminate a certain number of jurors for no specific reason (preemptory challenges).

It was so today when the trial of Ben, Sr.,

Butch and Jesse got underway. The judge was Robert F. Peckham. The prospective jurors were packed into the small federal courtroom waiting to be called when a postponement was announced early in the day. Butch was conferring with his attorney and his family.

Several hours later as court was convened, his attorney announced Butch would plead guilty to the bank robbery charge. Butch was removed from the trial and sentencing set for the end of the case.

That left only Ben, Sr. and Jesse, both of whom denied their guilt, as defendants. With Jesse's guilt obvious, all of the resources of the government were marshaled to seek a conviction on a bank robbery charge for the man who wasn't there that fateful November day.

April 11

The government established the basic facts of its case with bank officials, one of the women hostages, police and FBI Agent Joe Chiaramonte testifying. Pictures taken by automatic cameras inside the bank as well as by photographers at the time of the chase were introduced as evidence along with the weapons that were used.

There was very little cross-examination from the defense. Both Sam Cohen, representing Ben, Sr., and Harry Parker, appearing for Jesse, were appointed for the defendants because they are knowledgeable, experienced veterans of the courtroom. But there was not much to dispute at this point and they either asked no questions or merely clarified some details. They were both waiting for tomorrow.

Art was not in the courtroom. There was no reason for him to be. He was not on trial. He did drive to the court building in Ben, Jr.'s Grand Prix to confer with Mr. Ubhaus as the trial went on. He mingled very little with the spectators and, of the three defendants, saw only Butch.

But Art was very much present in terms of the evidence presented about the planning, the weapons, the robbery, the kidnaping and the chase. In fact, Cohen and Parker are doing their best to make sure it is as much a trial of Art as of their own clients.

April 12

At 11 A.M., following a short recess, U. S. Attorney Michael Fields announced he was calling his next witness. I left the courtroom, walked along the walkway to the public defender's office at the end of the building, and went in to the office where Mr. Ubhaus, Dan, and Art were waiting.

"They're ready," I announced. With that we walked quickly down the hall, past the relatives and friends of the accused, most of them well-known to Art, and into the courtroom. Mr. Ubhaus, Dan, and I sat down. Art stood by the door while a marshal directed him to the front of the bench. The clerk administered the oath. Art listened carefully to every word, his hand raised.

"Do you solemnly swear that the testimony you are about to give in this court shall be the truth, the whole truth and nothing but the truth, so help you God?"

"Yes," Art replied.

"You may take the stand. Please state your full name, address, and occupation for the record."

"My name is Arthur John DePeralta. I'm a student...."

Art was dressed in a sharply tailored double-knit blue suit with white pin-striping on the jacket. His black hair was neatly combed but sometimes fell loosely across part of his face. For the first time since last November he was face to face and only a few yards away from two of his partners in the robbery. They watched his every movement intensely.

Mr. Fields took him very carefully through all the details of the robbery itself, then got into the planning of the heist.

"When did you first meet Jesse?"

"About two years ago. He was messing around with this chick I knew. We partied a little bit, you know, went out and got loaded and stuff, and I didn't see too much of them for about a year until last summer."

"What happened last summer?"

"Jesse used to be over at Big Ben's house all the time. I'd go over there and get loaded with them, bullshit and kid around, you know, the normal stuff. Not really normal, but the stuff that you do when you party, get in fights and stuff like that. We did that once in a while during the summer whenever we ran into each other. Then, Jesse introduced me to Butch. He was around Big Ben's house a lot too. Then I didn't see them for a couple of months, something like that."

"What got you back in contact with them?"

"I read in the newspaper that Big Ben got shot in the leg and I called him and asked how he was doing, and he said he was all right. Then a couple of days later Butch and Jesse came over, and they asked me about if I wanted to make some money. First I asked how much, and they said about twenty-five thousand dollars. I was stunned. And, they told me what we had to do at first, and I was kind of hesitant about it."

"What did they tell you?"

"They told me we were going to rob a bank."

"Were any plans set at this time?"

"They told me that I was going to have to go in there and just watch the people while Jesse got the money, and Butch would come in the back door."

"Was Benny there at this time?"

"Benny was in the hospital during this time, but then before Benny got out of the hospital they kept on coming over and picking me up, and you know, they just clued me in more about the job."

"What were you to do in the bank?"

"They told me I was supposed to fire a shot and keep an eye on everybody, and after we did that I was to put everybody on the floor. Jesse told me to talk rough like we really meant business."

"Did you ever talk with Benny about the robbery?"

"Somewhat. Sunday while he was still in the hospital, Ben, Jr. took me to the hospital to see his father."

"Did Benny tell you how he got shot?"

"Yes, he said it was an accident. Nothing to worry about. He said he told the hospital the wound had come as a result of a fight with a guy over a television set."

"Did he say who shot him? Was anybody else there when you discussed this with Benny?"

"Yes. He shot himself. It was an accident with one of the guns he always keeps by him in his wheelchair. Butch and Jesse were there when Benny told me about it."

"What was the conversation with all of you at the hospital?"

"We were just talking about the job later on and I guess I was daydreaming about getting all that money. Benny gave us some money to get a lid of grass and party that night. He said he was going to get out of the hospital on Tuesday and we'd do the job then. He got out Tuesday, but he didn't get out at the time he expected to, so we just called it off until Wednesday. Then Wednesday came along and I cut school part of the day, and went over to Benny's house. Just Benny was there, so Benny said, "We'll do it tomorrow." Butch came by and got thirty dollars from Benny to buy a 12-gauge pump shotgun. The block had been taken out of it so it could hold more than three shots."

"What happened the night before, and the morning of the robbery?"

"Butch and Jesse came over and picked me up. We went and got loaded that night and tried to relax as much as possible for the next day. Thursday came around and we woke real fast, real early. Jesse and Butch split in Ben's green Chevy Impala to find a car for the job. They came back a little later and told me to get everything ready. Benny gave me my stocking, my gloves and Jesse handed me my gun. We got ready, smoked some more grass and got loaded, but I really couldn't get loaded because I was too nervous then. Then we left."

"At any time did Benny furnish any of the weapons?"

"That 9-millimeter and snub nose are Benny's guns."

"What did Benny do on Thursday morning?"

"He followed us in his car, and turned off at the expressway. There is a road in back of the bank by some apartments and Benny was supposed to be there. He had a 30-30 rifle with a scope. He was supposed to block off any cops who might try to come through the back way to the bank. That protection was important."

"Did you ever see Benny after he turned off

the expressway near the bank? Did you ever see him when you were at the bank?"

"No."

Mr. Fields concluded his examination of Art just in time for the noon recess.

At 1:45 P.M. the court reassembled. Art again took the stand, and Benny's lawyer began his cross-examination. The easy flow of the questions from the prosecutor quickly gave way to the biting, sometimes brutal attack of the defense. And the barrage was not long in coming.

"You hate Benny, don't you?"

"No, I do not."

"In fact, you were angry at him for several weeks before the robbery, is that not correct?"

"No, it isn't."

"And the reason you hate him is because he beat you up, worked you over pretty bad, didn't he?"

"He did not beat me up or work me over."

"And he beat you up because he wanted to stop you from having sexual intercourse with his niece. Isn't that true, Mr. DePeralta?"

"No, it isn't."

"You knew that Benny was in the hospital because he was shot. Is that correct?"

"Yes."

"And isn't it a fact that you knew he was shot because you shot him?"

"No, it is not a fact, and I did not shoot him."

"And isn't it true that Benny told you he made up the story about the argument over the television set with another man to protect you?"

"No, it is not true. He made the story up to

cover the fact he had the gun in the first place and then had shot himself."

There was medical testimony available that, if introduced, would have substantiated Art's statement that Big Ben's recent wound had been self-inflicted. That evidence was not called for.

The cross-examination then turned to the details of the robbery in the hope that Art would contradict what he had said during direct examination or get confused. Art remained remarkably calm during this ordeal, did not get angry in his responses, and most important, remained consistent in his testimony. The questioning by Benny's attorney turned finally to the statements Art had given the authorities.

"You gave several statements to the FBI at various times. Four to be exact. Right?"

"Yes."

"And did you tell the truth when you gave those statements?"

"Yes, I did."

"Yet nowhere in those first two statements does Benny's name appear, does it?"

"That is correct."

"But all at once in the third and fourth statements you talk a great deal about him planning the robbery. Correct?"

"Yes."

"And yet you say the statements are all true?"

"Yes, they are. The first two statements are true as far as they go. They say exactly what happened except for Benny's part. I left him out. I didn't want to bring him into it at first. Then later, after thinking it over, I did mention him."

"Why did you later mention him?"

"Because I decided to tell the full truth."

"Wasn't it really because you were angry at Benny, wanted to get even at him for beating you up, and in the process help your own case?"

"No."

At this point, Jesse's attorney took over the cross-examination and the blows continued coming. The attorney made every effort to imply Art had been given favors and help by the government in return for his testimony.

"You're out on a lowered bail of twenty-five thousand dollars. What was the original figure?"

"One hundred thousand dollars."

"Who got it lowered for you?"

"Mr. Ubhaus, my attorney."

"And who posted the lowered bond?"

"My parents put up their house as security."

"Have you ever held any jobs?"

"I worked at a service station for a while and did some roofing work last summer."

"Is that all the work you've done?"

"All that's legal."

"You never completed high school and yet you're now enrolled in college? Who arranged that?"

"My high-school counselor. He told me of a special program where students who reached eighteen years of age could go into college if it appeared they had the ability to do the work. He recommended me and the college accepted me."

"Haven't we seen you around the courthouse driving an expensive car several times? What kind of a car is it?"

"A Grand Prix, Pontiac."

"That's a beautiful suit you have on. Do you usually dress every day like that?"

"No."

"Who bought those clothes for you?"

"My mother."

"How do you usually dress?"

"I wear jeans and a sport shirt to school."

"When you were released you got into a new high school very quickly. Who arranged that for you? Who asked them to take you?"

"Gordon McLean of Campus Life."

"You testified for the government here today. What kind of promises have been made to get you on the witness stand?"

"None."

"Oh, come on now. You expect something for your efforts, don't you? You have been told the second charge, kidnaping, will be dropped, haven't you?"

"No. No one has talked to me about any deals being made, and my attorney says there have been none. Nobody has offered me anything."

"Well, you expect to get off easy because you testified, don't you?"

"No, I don't think so. I expect I'm going to prison."

"Well, don't you at least hope it will go better for you because you took the stand?"

"Well, yes."

Finally came the welcome statement, "No further questions." Art was excused.

Jimmy, Butch's younger brother, took the stand to place Butch, Jesse, Art and Benny together at the time details on the robbery were being worked out. He also recognized several guns as belonging to Benny.

But the hospital visits remained a crucial issue. The defense was contending there had been no visits. In fact, most of their efforts were aimed at establishing that point.

Jimmy, like Butch, had been out on his own since his early teen years. He idolized his older brother and hung around some with the same group. Jimmy had managed to avoid most of the trouble; in fact, he had recently joined the Army. He was on leave for the trial.

"I'm really bitter about what Butch got into, and with the people who got him into it," Jimmy explained outside the courtroom. "If Butch isn't here to testify, I'm going to because I know a lot of what went on. I hope I can help my brother by coming out with it."

And he did. Butch's young brother provided some of the most important testimony the government presented against Ben, Sr. Jimmy's testimony is a crucial part of the case.

A tense courtroom day is over.

April 16

The government has had a couple of setbacks in its presentation. Witnesses who were patients in the hospital or visiting at the time have not been able to definitely identify any of Benny's visitors. Without fully establishing those hospital visits where the robbery was discussed, the conviction of the mastermind could be in doubt. Something more is needed, and everyone senses it.

Mr. Ubhaus, as a public defender, doesn't usually assist the government with its cases. But today he and I had lunch with one person whose testimony, if he gives it, might make the difference. Later, Frank Bondonno, a young Christian attorney, met with the prospective witness and offered him full legal counsel and advice. Our witness is ready.

April 17

The United States rested its case. The defense presentation was surprisingly short—just two witnesses. The first was FBI Agent Chiaramonte, who explained some details on the evidence, confirmed Art's first statements omitting Benny's name, and clarified a minor contradiction in Art's testimony as to who sat in the front and back seats of the car on the way to the robbery. The other was Ben, Sr.'s mother.

Benny's mother, elderly, kindly, the lines from years of hard work on her face, a Bible in her hand, took the stand to say her son was home the day of the robbery, didn't go out at night, and could only drive a car with automatic transmission. She was a little confused on her dates and soon was excused.

That was the defense. Neither Jesse nor Benny took the stand. Defendants do not have to testify, and no inference of guilt can be drawn against them because they choose not to take the stand.

The prosecution then had an opportunity for rebuttal testimony, limited to refuting what the defense had presented. The U.S. attorney asked for a short recess and said he would call one witness. The defense was busy trying to find out who that witness was, and was concerned when it was found out. Once again Mr. Ubhaus' office had been used to keep a witness from possible unpleasant encounters in the lobby, and as we walked through the crowd into court there were more than a few surprised people.

The judge entered, the court came to order and the final witness was directed to the chair in the box near the judge.

Ben, Jr. had taken the stand. It was one of the hardest decisions of his life, to come into court and testify against his father. He wasn't eager to do it. He and his father have not been close, but neither are they enemies.

But Ben, Jr. believes in telling the truth. His Christian commitment certainly means that much to him. He is angry at what has been done to the young men who came under his father's influence. Art is his friend; indeed, he considers him a brother. He is dismayed that Art was encouraged to rob a bank. Now when his closest friend needed support to be believed, Ben, Jr. decided to give that help.

The questions were short and to the point.

"Did you see your father when he was in the hospital? And if so, when?"

"Yes, I think it was Sunday night, a few days before the bank robbery."

"Who was with you?"

"Art DePeralta."

"Was there any discussion at the hospital about the robbery?"

"They talked in general terms about something big coming off in a few days. They weren't specific. I didn't know what they were talking about?"

"Did your dad indicate how he had been shot?"

"Yes. He said he accidentally shot himself."

There it was, in a few short answers, the corroboration of what Art had stated about his being at the hospital.

During cross-examination the attempt was made to discredit Ben, Jr.

"Isn't it a fact that Art is your closest friend?"

"Yes."

"And it's also a fact you hate your father, isn't it?"

"No. We are not close friends and never really have been. I don't agree with what he's done, but I do not hate him."

"And did you and Art discuss his testimony and yours before you came to court today?"

"With Art? No, I didn't discuss it with him."

The testimony is all in. The trial is moving to a close.

April 18

Today the jury listened to the closing arguments of both the prosecutor and defense.

The government attorney opened with a factual account of the various incidents in the crimes charged, then carefully outlined the evidence presented that he believed had proven his case.

Ben, Sr.'s lawyer struck hard at the theme that the evidence simply did not prove his client participated in any way in the bank robbery. He cast aside Art's testimony as being self-serving and the result of a dislike for Big Ben. He reminded the jury the two sides do not start out even in a court contest. The defense must prove nothing, but the government must prove each and every allegation to the point of overcoming even a reasonable doubt. This, he maintained, the government had not done. Any doubt must be resolved in favor of the defendant with a not-guilty verdict. And that is exactly the verdict he sought.

There was some real interest in just what Jesse's attorney would argue in summation. Would he again turn the focus on the man who wasn't on trial, Art?

The answer wasn't long in coming.

"There is no doubt my client is guilty of bank robbery. You know it. I know it. He knows it. We frankly expect you to find him guilty on that charge. But what of the kidnaping charge with its maximum penalty of life imprisonment?"

As the attorney went on to argue the severity of a life sentence, the prosecutor objected. "Your honor, the matter of sentence is for the judge alone and is not the concern of the jury. I object to defense counsel appealing to the jury on the basis of a possible long sentence. That issue is not for them to consider."

The judge agreed, but the defense found another way to make the same argument.

"You see my client sitting here. And you saw Mr. DePeralta the other day on the witness stand. Both of these men went into a bank armed, both robbed it, both took hostages, both threatened the life and safety of others in a wild chase, and both were captured at the end. The only difference is my client had a bullet wound in his head. I'm not really complaining about that. He's lucky to be alive, and people who go into banks with guns must assume that risk. But look at the difference, now, ladies and gentlemen, between my client and Art DePeralta, two men who did exactly the same thing!

"Art drives to court in a Grand Prix, a big expensive car; my client comes chained to a United States marshal. Mr. DePeralta wears a nice blue suit with white pin-striping, while my client wears clothes provided in jail. Art goes to college every day, while Jesse sits in a small, maximum-security county jail cell. Art has his bail lowered so he can be released, while there is no hope of my client being freed.

"No wonder people say justice is blind! What a contrast, and between two men, mind you, who did commit the same crime!

"But let's go a little further. My client knows he's going to prison. Shouldn't Mr. DePeralta expect the same thing? Sure, he said on the stand here that's what he expects, but is it really? Why would he enroll in college and go to classes if he actually believed he was going to be locked up?

"No, ladies and gentlemen, Mr. DePeralta hasn't leveled with you. He knows something. He knows there's a deal been made, a good deal for him.

"And that's not wrong. If they offered my client a deal, I'd urge him to accept it and he probably would. But no, the deal is only for Art. He gets the favored treatment.

"I'll tell you what the deal is. The government is going to drop the second charge, kidnaping, against Mr. DePeralta. He knows it and his attorney knows it. Mr. Ubhaus has been here each day, but he hasn't taken the stand to deny any deal has been made. I wonder why. Mr. Ubhaus even let his client make a statement to the FBI and the government attorneys, and Mr. Ubhaus wasn't even there. Think of it! A lawyer letting his client talk to the government without that attorney present. If I did that, I would be charged with improper conduct before the bar association. But Mr. Ubhaus let his client talk freely because he knew there was nothing to worry about, everything was all set.

"I don't object. That's fine. All I ask you, ladies and gentlemen, is that you give to my client the same break Art is about to get. Find Jesse not guilty of kidnaping. Just remember, both men did the same thing."

In his final argument, the U.S. attorney quietly said the evidence of guilt was there, the facts spoke for themselves, and added there was at that time no deal on with Art, no charges dropped.

Further, he had said nothing to either Art or his attorney about dropping any charges.

Court adjourned for the day.

April 19

This morning the jury heard the judge's instruction. They were given the rules they were to use in evaluating all the testimony, viewing the exhibits and considering the arguments of counsel. The judge explained the law, but the jurors alone were to be the deciders of facts. They would conclude who was telling the truth, and they would determine guilt or innocence.

Their deliberations began at 10:50 A.M.

There is no way to know when a jury will come back with a verdict or what it will be. Many attorneys believe the longer a jury is out, the greater the dissent and the better for the defense. But no one can ever be sure.

The family and friends of the accused waited quietly and nervously in the corridor. Jesse and Ben, Sr. were taken back to the county jail nearby to await the decision. The judge was in his chambers.

The attorneys talked together, relieving the tension with a little mild humor, but mainly talking about ways they might have improved their presentations. Hindsight can be such a useless luxury.

There was word from the jury. No, not a verdict. They wanted several pieces of testimony reread to them. Everyone reassembled in court. Then out again for further deliberation.

Finally, after about four hours of consideration, they sent out word: We have a verdict.

The courtroom quickly filled. Jesse and Ben, Sr. were brought in by the marshals. Jesse was serious and, for the first time, seemed not to notice his family and friends. Ben, Sr., his muscular arms firmly guiding his wheelchair, smiled with what appeared to be confidence at his wife and mother.

When everyone was in place, the jury entered and handed their verdicts to the clerk. The judge opened and looked at the formal sheets that had been filled out, and then returned them to the clerk to be read.

"Ben, Sr. is guilty of armed bank robbery.

"Jesse is guilty of both armed bank robbery and kidnaping.

"Guilty on all counts."

Jesse hit his left fist into his right hand. Ben, Sr. only stared straight ahead.

At the request of the defense attorneys, the jury was polled. So twice, one for each defendant, every juror responded, "This is my verdict."

The jury was excused with a word of grateful appreciation from the judge, and they were told they were at liberty to discuss the case or not, with anyone, as they might choose.

One of the jurors I talked with explained the verdict. "It really came down to whether we could believe Mr. DePeralta. When young Ben testified, we then believed DePeralta had been at the hospital. From that point we believed everything he said about the robbery. There was simply no really effective denial from the other side."

Believing Art was one thing, but liking him was another. A number of the jurors considered him as much a hood as those on trial.

Aside from the families and friends of the accused, there was someone else I knew would be interested in the verdict: Art. So I drove out to his house to give him and his family the news.

There was no elation, just relief that the trial was over, and sorrow that the whole tragedy had ever happened.

We went out for a drive to talk about it. Art was depressed. Though he had not heard the closing argument of Jesse's attorney, he echoed the same sentiments the lawyer had expressed.

"I'm no better than those guys. We all did the same thing. I haven't asked for anything special, but things *have* gone better for me. I've been trying to do what is right and I told the truth, but I don't deserve any more or any less than what they get. God loves me... well, He loves them too, doesn't He? Then why do I get the breaks, man, why? Why do people feel sorry for me? What about Big Ben in that wheelchair and Jesse with the bullet hole in his head and partly blind? How about them?"

I was dealing with a frustrated young man, and I had learned long before to answer him in direct terms.

"I don't know anyone who feels sorry for you. I don't. And I can't think of a reason anyone should. If there's anybody to feel sympathy for in all of this, it's those bank tellers you took as hostages and scared half to death. Then, I might have some sympathy left for Jesse with his wound and Big Ben in that chair. In fact, for almost anybody but you!

"Why the differences, you ask. God loves them just as He does you or anyone, but God's love must be received and responded to before it is operative in our lives. We must accept Christ, turn from our old ways, submit to His control, seek His guidance. You've done that. Sure, you

124

still have a long way to go, but you've started. And that's why God has worked in your life. You got into school, worked with Campus Life and your church, did some things to straighten out your life, and whether you like it or not, that can't help but make a difference in what becomes of you.

"You told the truth. Nothing more, nothing less. You didn't ask for any deals; you didn't try to get anybody; you simply answered the questions with the truth. And that has made a difference.

"You're trying, learning, building, growing, maturing, and much as it may upset you at the moment, it has changed you. I know you're sorry about all this progress, but you're stuck with it!"

Art said nothing for a long time, just kept driving. When we pulled up into his driveway, he turned to me and said, "I want you to promise me something."

"What's that?"

"That you'll pray for Butch, Jesse and Big Ben. Will you?"

"Yes."

With that, he got out and went in the house.

April 20

I talked with Mr. Ubhaus this morning.

"That was quite a summation from Jesse's lawyer," Art's attorney commented. "Especially that part about all the deals for Art. I wish everything were sewed up that easy. We've had no promises, but I'll tell you this, as long as everybody thinks the kidnaping charge will be dropped, that's exactly what I'm going to ask for!"

April 22

This morning we met with two catchers from the California Angels, Jeff Torborg and John Stephenson, along with utility infielder Jerry DaVanon. They're excited about starting chapel programs on the road for their team. Art was again tremendously impressed by the warmth and dedication of the athletes.

Prior to the game, the Oakland A's sponsored an Easter service for their fans. About ten thousand were there. They heard Jim Shofner, a coach with the San Francisco 49'ers football team, Minnesota Viking Jeff Siemon, high-school coach Ben Parks and others sharing their Christian faith. The featured speaker was Bobby Richardson, formerly with the Yankees and now coaching at the University of South Carolina. I also had a part in the program.

While it was going on, Art was a guest of the Angels in the locker room, came with them to the service, and added another signed baseball to his collection.

April 24

This morning Art went before the federal judge to enter his plea. Before the court appearance, Mr. Ubhaus carefully reviewed once again all that was involved.

"You have a right to a trial," Mr. Ubhaus told him, "to have the evidence of your guilt produced in court, and to have your side presented. Then you can only be convicted if all twelve jurors agree. Should you be found guilty, you have a right to appeal the case. If you plead guilty, there will be no trial and no right to appeal. You will give up all of those rights. The only question then will be one of the sentence."

Art understood fully and indicated he would enter the guilty plea. In court, the judge went to extra lengths to be sure the young defendant fully understood all of his rights and that Art's decision was being freely made.

"Did anyone make any threats or promises to get you to plead guilty?" the judge asked him.

"No, sir," Art replied, dressed neatly in a blue suit and standing with his counsel before the bench.

"Were any promises made as to what the sentence would be if you do plead guilty? Do you understand that the matter of sentence is my decision alone, and until I've read the probation report I have no idea as to what that sentence will be? The maximum sentence for bank robbery is twenty-five years in prison and a ten thousand dollar fine."

Each time Art indicated that he fully understood.

"Is there anyone you are covering up for or hiding in their guilt by your plea?"

"No, sir."

Mr. Ubhaus advised the court that the government had agreed to drop the kidnaping charge and to send a letter to the parole authorities advising of Art's cooperation. That agreement had been made four days prior to this court session. Other than that, there were no promises.

"Then, Mr. DePeralta," concluded the judge, "you are entering your plea of guilty because in fact you are guilty of the crime of armed bank robbery and for no other reason. Is that correct? And you are satisfied with the legal counsel that you have had in this case?"

To both questions Art answered, "Yes, sir."

The judge ordered the guilty plea entered in the record and asked for a probation report before sentencing.

The U.S. attorney then moved for dismissal of the second count, kidnaping, and indicated the government had no objection to Art remaining free on bail.

Later in the day, Butch, who was to have driven the getaway car, came before the same judge for sentencing and received a ten-year commitment under the Youth Corrections Act. This is a federal law aimed at rehabilitating young offenders; it carries no set minimum sentence, allows for release at any time the authorities feel the person is ready to return to the community, and eventually permits the conviction to be set aside. It was a generous disposition for Butch.

Butch indicated he felt he had gotten a good

break when we talked after court. "It could have been much worse," he commented, obviously relieved. "I want to do my own time, keep my nose clean and get out. I just hope I don't get in any more trouble."

The choice was his, I assured him. And if he took full advantage of the break he'd been given, coupled with a realistic look at his relationship with the Lord, there was no reason he could not make it.

"I was once close to the Lord," Butch responded, "but then things just seemed to get all messed over and I got away from Him."

"Whose fault was that?" I asked.

"Mine," he honestly responded.

"That's right, Butch. If a guy doesn't feel close to God, guess who moved."

I assured him we'd see he got *Campus Life* magazine regularly and a *Reach Out*, and would certainly pray for him and keep in contact. We'd also give any help we could to his younger brothers.

"Remember, Butch, you can't do anything about your past, but the future is a different story. Today is the first day of the rest of your life. Make it good."

"I want to very much," he replied. "Let's keep in touch. And tell Art I wish him well."

I passed the word to Art this evening when we met for some Bible study at Ben, Jr.'s apartment.

April 29

Aside from adding another autographed baseball to his growing collection, Art scored another first today. He recorded an interview with Brooks Robinson, veteran third baseman of the Baltimore Orioles, to use as part of our talk show tonight. The subject will be the future of baseball and some of the problems of our national sport.

"This really blew my mind," Ben, Jr., who came along with us, commented after the game. "I never thought I'd get to know some of the big league players like Brooks. He's a very down-to-earth guy and a real Christian. That's wild, man."

May 2

The probation officer preparing a pre-sentence report for the judge talked with Art today and later visited his home.

Before their meeting, Art was not too eager to undergo another interrogation. "I just don't want to answer any more questions for anybody," he said quite emphatically. Mr. Ubhaus reminded Art that this interview was important and could have a great deal to do with the recommendation the probation officer would make to the court. So Art kept the appointment. After it was over, he seemed reasonably happy about the whole thing.

"There's just a lot of things bugging me lately and I'm sorry I get uptight. The P.O. seems all right, wanted to know what I had to say, and I think he'll treat me okay," Art commented.

Later today Art talked with his girl friend for awhile, then stopped by my apartment after the college group meeting at his church. The buddy who came over with him is no stranger to the kinds of trouble Art has been in. He was in on some of it, but now he's got his head together pretty well, holds a steady job, and is helping his family. The guys joined John Hafner, Dan and me in some fellowship and study.

May 5

The magazine article was about the Watergate break-in, hidden funds, and unreported political campaign contributions. Art read intently as we ate breakfast.

"What gives with these guys?" he asked angrily, looking up from the page. "They got all the money they need, so why do they have to go around pulling jobs? What are they trying to prove? Are they just a bunch of two-bit hoods in good clothes?"

Those were questions not easy to answer. I suggested to Art that, at the time of the break-ins, they felt they were saving the country from some kind of radical takeover.

"Does that mean if you think what you're after is right, then it doesn't make any difference what you do or how you get it?" Art asked, probing deeper. "Is that how these burglars, and the people who got them to do the jobs, figured it?"

"That's about it," I responded, as disgusted as Art.

"Maybe I should tell the judge I robbed the bank to help the country, you know, to get more money in circulation, or something," Art added sarcastically.

"Then here's a story on a big federal judge who is supposed to have taken two hundred eighty-five thousand dollars to help some race track operation when he was a state governor. He gets three years in the joint but it says here he may not serve any of it. At that rate nobody on our job should get any more than sixteen months. We got out and used guns and at least people knew we were crooks. These other guys dress good, have big jobs, are supposed to be great leaders and then pull off all sorts of rip-offs. Stealing is stealing, ain't it?"

"Yes, it is," I agreed. "You know, Art, if you feel strongly about this kind of thing, perhaps you should go into politics."

"No way!" Art countered.

May 6

The Chicago Cubs played a doubleheader in Oakland today. Art and Ben, Jr. were the guests of Randy Hundley, another Christian athlete. Both continue to be encouraged as they learn of the stand taken for the Lord by men who make sports headlines.

After they returned, Art and I had a chance to talk about his future.

"I don't look forward to being locked up, but if that's what should happen, then I'll make the best of it. I hope I can get into a program where I can study some of the things I'm interested in, even get some credits I can transfer to college when I come home.

"When I come back I'd like to work perhaps in the auto mechanic field for awhile, get a car of my own and an apartment. Then I hope to go on to college, working my way through. I'm not really sure just what it is I want to do in the long run, but I think I'd like to help people. Even with a job, I hope I can help Campus Life with kids at Juvenile Hall or the county ranch so they don't go on into more trouble. My experience might be able to help some of them."

Art seems to accept his fate as far as confinement is concerned, and his plans for the future appear to be realistic. I suggested some things he will have to learn if he is going to reach those goals.

First, he will have to start saying *no* to himself. If he wants a good job and further education, it will take considerable effort. He'll have to choose what he *should do* instead of settling for what he *wants* to do. Fun will have to give way to hard work and studies. There is no question as to his *ability*; his *dependability* will make the difference.

Second, he'll have to accept people more readily. Art has made some good progress in this area, but he still has barriers between himself and the people who have used and misused him. He often keeps friends at a distance and tends to see people in terms of his own personal advantage, which is exactly the complaint he registers against those who misguided him.

I talked to Art about his habit of testing limits and friendships. "How far can I go without really blowing it?" seems to be his guideline. He often does things to anger a person, thus proving to his own satisfaction that they really don't like him after all.

Third, he needs to learn how to manage money. Even more than those who work, people who get their money illegally usually squander it as fast as it comes. Restraint, savings and waiting are words just now creeping into Art's vocabulary. He will also have to learn the importance of giving to God and sharing with others as part of Christian responsibility.

You've probably noticed that the things pointed out here are not limited to a reformed bank robber. If Art needs to learn them, there is one consolation. He has lots of company.

May 8

"It's a good thing we left our arsenal outside or we'd have been dead now and so would some cops."

The seventeen-year-old youth sitting across from Art and me at Juvenile Hall hardly looked like the type to make such a threat, but Jack was not kidding. A few days before, he and his older partner had been busted for six armed robberies as police burst into their apartment and seized the unarmed suspects.

Jack explained what had happened. "My partner had shot off one of our guns the day before and it had gone through the wall into the next apartment. We decided to stash our pieces (guns) outside in case the cops came snooping around. Well, they came all right, but it was to bust us for the robberies. They grabbed my partner in the hallway, then found me asleep in the bedroom. I awoke staring into the muzzle of an M-16 rifle being held by a cop who left no doubt he was ready to use it. There were six other armed cops in the room. I was the most cooperative boy you ever saw!"

Good-looking, well-built, neat, extremely intelligent, polite—all are descriptives given of Jack by many people who knew him, not counting, of course, those who met him when he was wearing a disguise, carrying a .357 Magnum, and robbing them. One of his victims had a particular reason for remembering Jack. When the old man dared the robbers to shoot him and Jack's partner was about ready to oblige, Jack stepped between them and knocked out the victim with a heavy blow from the gun. That incident added an assault with a deadly weapon charge to the list.

Jack's attorney is Joe Silva and the big battle ahead in the courts is to get Jack sent to a youth facility instead of state prison.

Jack's prior juvenile history, by the way, consisted of two referrals, one for running away from home and the other for hitchhiking on a freeway. Off the record, he had done considerable stealing and used a variety of drugs, stopping just short of heroin and the needle.

He had run away from home wanting freedom from parental control and the boredom of school. He also had a lengthy list of grievances against society as a whole and thought he and his friends were the ones to set the world right. When none of this seemed too successful, he joined the service but was quickly discharged when they learned of his drug use.

He wasn't about to go home and settle down to the dull routine of school, home, and old buddies. It was much more exciting to be out on his own, look for work, meet older friends and, to quote him, "live a little." At a boarding house where he stayed, Jack met a security guard interested in beating the systems of companies like the ones for which he worked. For a partner the guard needed an impulsive young man with not the best judgment but plenty of nerve. Jack fit the bill and they were soon in business hitting liquor stores and restaurants.

After job number six, the police caught up with the pair and Jack was placed in Juvenile Hall. However, he may be tried as an adult because of his age, maturity, and his living away from his family.

During our conversation we learned Jack was no stranger to church, in fact he held a position of leadership in his parish assisting the pastor in the liturgy at services. A personal relationship with the Lord? Now that was something else again. Jack knew little about such an experience.

Jack and Art have many similarities in their background and current situations, enough at least so Jack listened carefully as Art told of his experiences in trouble, in the courts, and in rebuilding his life in the six months he has been awaiting the climax of the court case.

For his part, Jack readily admitted he was in deep trouble with problems he could not handle. "I tried telling myself I was too smart, too good a shot, and too fast a runner to ever be caught. Deep inside I knew better. But the deeper I got in the hole I was digging, the more hopeless everything seemed. I know I'm going to be locked up for a long time; that's not what worries me. I'm just wondering if there is any way I can change from the kind of person I've been."

There was a good answer to that question, and Art was an appropriate man to share it. He did, telling Jack of a commitment to the Lord that went far beyond religious form or tradition.

"I see what you're driving at and it sounds okay," Jack responded, "but there's an awful lot going through my head right now. I need some time to fit all the pieces together."

No doubt Jack has a long way to go in solving his problems. He's certainly smart enough to think things through carefully, and he has a family that is very much concerned for him.

He still could make something of his future. But only if he's wise enough to admit he can't do it all alone.

May 9

It is not always easy to know the results when Art, or anyone, shares personal experiences with a group, on television, radio, or in print. People may say they enjoyed it, but was anybody *really* helped?

Today a young lady sent Art a serious letter. She knows something about problems and discouragement; her own father has been in prison.

"I've read about what happened to you, first the bad and now some good things," she wrote. "It has been a real help to me. I had doubts about God making a difference in our lives, or even if He existed. I really know better, but it's so easy to ask questions when things are going wrong.

"The change in your life has been a real encouragement to me, a reason to have some hope, because I am sure it has not been easy for you getting started in a new life. Your experience has helped me believe God can straighten out my problems. I've gotten enough of whatever it takes to start praying for my own needs, and I plan to include you, too, in my prayers."

Perhaps such a letter is just an adolescent diversion. But not necessarily. It may well result from the impact the life of one young person has on another, a sharing that builds. If so, it worked both ways. Her letter meant much to Art.

May 11

Jesse awaits sentencing in the maximum security jail cell where he has been confined since his transfer from the prison hospital.

There are a total of eleven brothers and sisters in his family; Jesse is the youngest of the boys. They are close to each other. As he is expecting the worst in court, he has asked his family not to be present next Monday. But a number of them will come anyway, including his mother.

Jesse writes his feelings about "people dying of starvation, others being murdered by their own hatred, or dying from drinking and drugs. This is the path I was heading to, so you'll see even though I am in prison I feel glad in a way, because now I may learn to be more considerate and understanding. I was living the life of a hood because I was ignorant of reality.

"In this jail you meet some people who hate their families and this country. I feel we're fortunate to live in this land because a lot of countries are having wars. It's miserable to see people dying from bullets and little children starving. That's what I remember from the service.

"I want to change the way I feel about life in general because I was wasting mine. I'd like to live the life the Lord meant for us to live. I didn't, and that's the reason I'm so miserable.

"My mind really goes through some weird changes, but it's about time I finally decided to make a change. Sometimes I feel like crying for being such a fool."

Here is a bitter, confused young man, groping for release from the anger inside him, yet apparently not able to cut loose from the damning emotional hold of Big Ben. No wonder Jesse continues to be frustrated at every turn as his problems get bigger and, in his mind, more hopeless.

Unfortunately, I doubt if either the tragedies in Jesse's life or the grief of his family have ended. As long as he and Benny are together, even in jail, there may well be more difficulties ahead.

May 13

Tomorrow Art, Jesse and Ben, Sr. will be sentenced in federal court. I got to thinking today about how hard that must be for a conscientious judge.

Judge Marvin Frankel, in his book *Criminal Sentences*, says, "It is our duty to see that the force of the state, when it is brought to bear through the sentences of our courts, is exerted with the maximum we can muster of rational thought, humanity, and compassion." But judges are lawyers; no page in a law book can tell them how to deal with the variables of human nature.

Many citizens cry only for punishment—the longer the better. Yet judges know what that does to a man and how often the ex-convict coming out of prison is in worse moral shape than when he went in, despite the institution's attempts to help him. If he gets into trouble again, the public says, "See?" and refuses all the more to give the sincere ex-con a job or a second chance.

Yet society has to be protected, too. There are no easy answers.

May 14

The sentencing calendar began in court with a motion by Jesse's lawyer for a new trial. He argued that a reference to another bank robbery during the trial had prejudiced the minds of the jurors.

Big Ben's attorney asked for a new trial based on a failure to give his client a trial separate from the other defendants.

Both motions were denied.

Big Ben, speaking on his own behalf, told the courtroom he was not guilty of the charges and said he would appeal the verdict. The court informed Benny that that was his privilege and explained briefly the procedure.

The U.S. attorney recommended a maximum sentence for Benny based on his four previous felony arrests and his leading younger men into crime.

The judge agreed strongly. "You are a Fagin who planned and instigated criminal actions carried out by other young men who were, to various degrees, influenced by you," he told the man in the wheelchair. "You have already paid dearly for your life of crime, disabled by the bullets of police in another country. While you did not go into the bank or detain hostages, you were the dominant figure in setting up the crime."

The sentence was twenty-five years.

Then Jesse's case was called. His attorney asked the court to accept the probation department recommendation that his client be given a suspended sentence on the kidnaping charge. He also informed the court that several jurors who heard the case wanted to recommend leniency for Jesse in view of the treatment they expected Art to receive.

"This may be a serious case, your honor, but the fact remains that to this day another defendant accused of doing what my client did walks the streets a free man with every expectation he will get a break when he comes before this court."

His attorney told how Jesse had volunteered for military service, but then got involved with drugs, had marital problems, couldn't find work when he returned home and finally gave up hope. He said Jesse had made every effort to cooperate with the government, offered to plead guilty and would have testified if needed.

The U.S. attorney denied that such an arrangement was considered.

"I felt I had a drug problem from the service," Jesse said when it came his turn to speak. "When I came back from military duty, things were changed. It was hard to get a job."

"Your prior record is not a long one," the judge finally told him. "But the crime and the circumstances both make the offense a grave one. It is just the grace of God that the hostage you held was not hurt or killed, or a police officer. No matter what made you the person you are today, I can only conclude that you are a menace to society and would be a threat to the safety of many people if you were released. You must be incarcerated—and for a substantial time."

The sentence was thirty years for kidnaping, twenty-five for bank robbery, to run concurrently.

Court recessed for lunch.

Two U.S. marshals took Benny, Jesse and a young defendant from another case in a marshal's private car and headed for the county jail a few blocks away. Just as they pulled away from the court building, Benny, who was not handcuffed, used a karate chop to overpower the marshal driving and seized his gun.

"Do what we tell you or you're a dead man!" said the defiant convict.

Then Benny learned that the marshal sitting with Jesse had put a second weapon in the trunk. The two marshals were ordered out of the car and the three felons, now armed with a gun, sped away.

A plainclothes officer driving by noticed the men being pushed from the car, made a quick U-turn and began pursuing. The chase moved through city streets and into a parking lot where the two vehicles snaked between lines of trucks and automobiles. A road grader barely crawled out of their way. Suddenly Benny headed straight for a chain-link fence and, without slowing down, burst through the barrier, ripping out thirty feet of fencing.

He turned too wide at the next corner, however, swerved into a parked car and came to a jolting stop. The three were quickly captured and taken to their original destination, the county jail. Now Benny will get slapped with charges of escape, assault on a federal officer and using a gun to commit a felony. Jesse will be charged with escape.

Unaware of all this, Art, his family and girl friend arrived at court for his sentencing. They were quickly brought into the court building and told of the escape. Most of the court people were shocked, but Art himself was not really surprised.

When court reassembled somewhat later than

scheduled, it was with an air of tension and under tightened security.

The U.S. attorney indicated he would make no recommendation in Art's case, but noted that Art had pleaded guilty and testified for the government at the recently completed trial.

Mr. Ubhaus spoke for Art. "Here is a young man who six months ago was going nowhere but downhill with his life. He participated in a serious, dangerous criminal act. Since his release and in the time I have known him, he has shown genuine remorse for his actions. He has accepted the limitations placed on him by order of the court and has cooperated fully. Beyond that, it is obvious to everyone here and to much of the community that this young man has made strong progress in rehabilitating himself. He has participated in a number of worthwhile activities, done it sincerely, and has gone far beyond what a man would do if he were only trying to impress a sentencing judge. He has helped other young people and involved himself in the most useful of community and Christian activities."

"That is true," the judge noted, "but don't forget this young man also held a loaded gun to the head of a terrified hostage and forced her to drive a car around the city for forty-five minutes—after he had committed the largest bank robbery in the history of the area.

"Is there anything you would like to say?" the judge asked Art.

"Yes," said Art, speaking slowly and quietly, "I am very sorry for the trouble I've caused my family and everyone else. In a way, I'm glad I was caught, in the sense that it made me take a look at where I was heading. And my life has changed out of the experience. That is something good that came from it. But I'm still sorry for all the innocent people I hurt."

The judge invited me to address the court on my experiences with Art. Earlier, I had provided the judge with a written summary of our work with Art. Standing with Art and Mr. Ubhaus, I again pointed out my belief in the sincerity of the young man, his desire to rebuild his life, the progress he had made and our willingness to work with him now and in the future.

Then the judge announced his decision.

"Sentencing you, Mr. DePeralta, presents a difficult problem and conflict for the court. You committed a very serious crime; you were playing for high stakes. You risked other people's lives as well as your own in a series of dangerous actions. On the other side, you were only seventeen at the time of this robbery. You have been most contrite and obviously acting in good faith since that time. Your testimony has been helpful to the government and you have told the truth about what you have done. That is in your favor. The real test, of course, has yet to come as to what you will do in the future, and I hope you'll be successful.

"But this court cannot grant probation, not for a crime this serious. The sentence I am imposing will be fashioned in such a way as to help you and to encourage you to make progress in the future.

"I hope you do not leave this room bitter. There is no need for that. If you keep going on in the right direction, and I believe that is what

149

you want to do, you will have the opportunity to show that and to gain an early release.

"I am going to sentence you under provisions of the Youth Corrections Act, which carries no minimum sentence. You may be released anytime federal parole authorities feel you should be released. Later, your conviction on this charge can be set aside.

"The sentence will be ten years."

The length of sentence came quickly and almost as an anticlimax. Some of the audience whispered to ask, "How long did he say?" Others heard it and sighed, some in relief, others in reaction to what they considered a long time, even if deserved, for such a young man.

Art himself was sober, moved, but not distressed. It was what he had expected.

He was released pending assignment to the designated correctional facility, and will report there on his own.

Outside the courtroom, a woman stopped Art. "It was my daughter you held as a hostage," she informed him.

"Tell her I'm very sorry for what happened. I do intend to make something good out of my life in the future," Art replied.

"Good luck, young man," said the woman. She shook his hand and left.

May 21

Before Jesse left his cell he was searched, given new clothes, handcuffed and manacled—even though, as was the case today, he was going only to the attorneys' visiting room inside the jail. His keepers were taking no chances of a repeat escape attempt.

His chains clanking, he fumbled for a cigarette, dropped it, then picked it up and lit it.

"What in the world happened last week?" I asked.

"I don't know," he replied, shaking his head. "It wasn't planned; it just happened.

"Benny grabbed the marshal in the front seat, and in a few seconds the two marshals were out of the car and Benny was behind the wheel taking off.

"I know this has fouled things up." He was right.

"I've never wanted to hurt anybody and I know there's no future in crime. I'd just like to get my medical treatment completed, do my time and get out to be with my wife and son.

"Maybe, with God's help, I can do that someday."

I told him God was a pretty good place to start rebuilding.

"I think a lot of people have the wrong idea about me. I had no intention of hurting the hostages in the bank. I'm not all rough and bad."

"People will find that hard to believe," I responded. "Neither the robbery conviction nor the escape charge do much good for your reputation." He nodded solemnly.

Switching topics, Jesse asked me to give his

best wishes to Art along with the hope that things would work out well for him. He hoped Art didn't hold any resentments because they had been left in the bank. I replied that Art was probably bitter at first, but tended to be much more understanding now. Jesse was glad Art was "into the Christ trip; it'll do the guy good. He's not really a bad kid. He just grew up too fast."

"Yes, and with the wrong people," I added. Big Ben had just passed by in his wheelchair and waved.

Jesse was interested in my book about Art and thought it might help young people.

"Tell those kids it's hard to start over like I'm going to have to do. Having your name all over page one so your family is hurt and then sitting here in chains when they come to see you is no picnic. Some easy, dishonest money, even a lot of it, isn't worth it. So many innocent people you really love get hurt when you blow it. You don't often see that at the time, but it can hit pretty hard when you're where I am.

"My biggest wish is to keep things together with my wife. She's taking some college classes and getting ready for a good position."

"Doing what?" I asked.

Jesse smiled. "She wants to be a police officer."

May 29

The two weeks since his sentencing have been busy ones for Art. Many people have seen, called or written him to wish him well. It's meant much to him.

"Go ahead and have me speak at any meetings you want," he told me a few days after court. "At least now no one will say I'm talking to try and influence my sentence. That is all over."

Art met with a reporter so the local press could update its story on him, take some pictures and publish the material they had been holding since before his trial. He taped a television special for later release, was on radio, and took part in a collegiate Christian conference. He spent time with his family and friends, helped one of my associates move, rebuilt my waterbed frame, and talked with two of Jesse's sisters who came to my office. (He also got a speeding ticket.)

I think back with amazement on this whole experience. When I took on Art's supervision at the request of the court I had no idea the project would be this long or involved. Not that it would have made much difference. To have ignored him would have negated all I believe about Christian involvement and concern. I did what I had to do, and beyond that, I look back and realize it has been a good experience for both of us.

Art is not the same young man I met in custody six months ago. He is more friendly, relaxed, caring and realistic. His barriers to people are coming down; his ability to accept and be accepted is stronger. As the judge stated, if it were not for the seriousness of the crime, Art would be a good prospect for probation.

Art's mother and stepfather are concerned for his future. "They have assured me of their love and support," Art told a newspaper reporter. "I think we are closer now than we have ever been. But they also feel I have done wrong and must pay for it, so they accept my being locked up."

Today Art goes behind bars.

"I deserve what I got," he said on the television program. "I want to get all the good education and training from the place I'm sent. I can also develop my attitude, work on my temper, set some goals and get at some of my hang-ups. It won't be a snap facing all those things but I have to and I will.

"I'm not bitter, even at Butch and Benny for leaving us at the bank. I've thought a lot about that and, if I'd been in their place, I'd probably have done the same thing. I don't want to look back at my past, but rather to what is up ahead."

What's going to happen to Art? When will he be released and, more important, what kind of person will he be then?

No one knows.

He has changed and is changing. In our daily contacts I have seen God molding Art's life into something worthwhile. He's not perfect yet, mind you, but so very far advanced from what he was when we met.

I know the institution, its staff, program, problems (like racial tensions behind the locked doors), and especially its inmates will have a strong influence on the future of this young man. Being locked up could undo much of what has been accomplished with Art. I hope not.

The choice of direction will be Art's. About all I can do now is pray for him.

Art told his family, girlfriend, and buddies good-bye this morning. He was nervous, yet reasonably cheerful, about his first airplane ride, a flight that would take him to prison.

May 31

I found out what happened when Art landed in an unfamiliar part of the country. No one met him at the airport, so he had to convince the airport security police that he indeed belonged at the nearby federal institution and needed a ride.

"But where is your guard?" asked the suspicious officer.

"There is no guard. I came here on my own," Art replied.

"You mean they took you out of jail, put you on a plane and sent you here alone?" the officer gasped. He couldn't imagine an eighteen-year-old flying many miles by himself to surrender and serve a ten-year sentence.

Art's answers only added to the bewilderment. "I wasn't in jail, I was home. The court told me when to come, gave me some papers and a ticket, and here I am."

"What did you do?"

"You may not believe this . . . ," and then Art told him. "Now as a policeman," Art concluded, "surely you believe that someone who did that should be locked up. And as soon as you get me a ride, I will be!"

That did it. Art got his ride.

He was driven to the institution, surrendered himself and was admitted. The door behind him was firmly locked.

May it be the last one.

A Personal Message from Art DePeralta

In this book you've read what happened to me and learned something of the kind of person I was.

Early in life I learned to live by my wits because I figured I needed to in order to survive. I was greedy because it was the fastest and easiest way to get what I wanted. I learned how to fight, steal and lie because I figured it was me against the world and that was the only way for me to win.

Of course I was wrong, and all of this combined to get me into big trouble with no apparent way out.

Then I met a Person who changed me in so many ways, Jesus Christ. Frankly, this talk about forgiveness didn't mean much when I first read *The Way* in my Juvenile Hall cell after I was arrested. I needed to be forgiven all right, but I was sure it would never happen to me. God might forgive some people, but not someone who had done as much wrong as I had.

You can imagine my amazement when I discovered He really can and will forgive when we ask. Obviously a man who is drowning doesn't argue too long with someone who wants to rescue him, and that was about my position. To be honest, forgiving myself for what I've done wrong to other people has been much harder than accepting Christ's pardon, but I'm working on it.

I want to make something of my life and my future. I want to help people instead of hurting them. I want to earn my way instead of stealing.

I didn't change to that view all by myself. A courtroom or cell didn't scare me into it. The Lord finally got through to a belligerent, stubborn guy. That made the difference.

Believe me, I've got a long way to go. I'm not perfect or even the straightest guy you'll meet. I blow it every now and then, and I sometimes get discouraged. I'm not all I ought to be, but I can assure you of this: I'm certainly not what I used to be!

Some good people don't trust me for what I did wrong. I expect that. Many of my old crowd hate me for what I've tried to do right, like telling the truth.

Those are a couple of my battles. But with a lot of good friends behind me I'll make it. More important, God is still working on me, and that means a lot.

But what about you? I'm confident enough from what the Lord has done in my life to recommend Him for your needs, even if you never committed a major crime.

Whatever you may think of Art DePeralta when you finish this book isn't really all that important. What you *do* about accepting the Lord is.

He wants you very much.

Now.

How about it?

Above: Police finally pin the green Chevrolet against a telephone pole outside San Jose.
Below: Hostage Nancy Valentine watches from the driver's seat while police maneuver; Art, Jesse, and Hostage Mrs. Linda Starkey are all crouching out of view.

Above: Miss Valentine escapes the car as Art comes out with hands up.

Below: Police wrestle Art to the ground.

The next day's headlines.

Art DePeralta